What People are Saying

We are living in a rare moment in time where law and order and plain decency are on their heads. The weaponization of the media following the Solomon Asch experiments has us believing that the sun shines brightest at midnight. Dr. Bart Billings has witnessed the evolution of the media and its evil intents, which he explains in this new book, a must read! —**Mark L. Gordon, MD Medical Director, Millennium's Veteran TBI Program, Magnolia, Texas**

The media has become a highly toxic infestation of contaminated life-altering events that has caused an intrusive and invasive brainwashing in today's youths, while generating multiple puncture wounds, which is damaging our Country's society and is on the verge of fracturing our freedom. Dr. Bart Billings is a true American professional who has brought to life an exceptional story describing how our nation is crumbling before our eyes. —**William H. LaBarge, USN (Ret) Navy Carrier Pilot, Commercial Airline Captain, and New York Times Bestselling Author**

Dr. Billings's book sheds light on what is happening to our country through media empire wars. His abundant knowledge, with six decades of honorable service, including the military, the health field, and media, speak volumes in his naked truth book exposing how the "Google = Goebbels" media machine is covertly transforming America into a National Socialist Democratic party. —**John J. Cooper USAF Strategic Air Command, GS-12 Dept. of Defense, RedCross Ukraine** ❖

HOW THE MEDIA CREATES VICTIMS IN OUR SOCIETY

Building castles on the bones of the people they sacrifice

Bart P. Billings, Ph.D.

© 2024 Bart P. Billings, Ph.D. All rights reserved.

Published by DP Diversified
a division of DocUmeant Publishing
244 5th Avenue, Suite G-200
NY, NY 10001
646-233-4366

No part of this book may be reproduced in any form or by any electronic or mechanical means, including information storage and retrieval systems, without permission in writing from the publisher, except by a reviewer who may quote brief passages in a review.

The publisher has used its best efforts in preparing this book, and the information provided herein is provided "as is".

The views expressed in this book are solely those of the author and do not necessarily reflect the views of the publisher.

The author has attempted to recreate events, locales, and conversations from their memories of them. Some names and identifying details may have been changed to protect the privacy of individuals.

Editor Anne C. Jacob of Popin Edits
AnneCJacob.com

Cover design by Todd Fishback

Book design and production by Ginger Marks of DocUmeant Designs
DocUmeantDesigns.com

Library of Congress Control Number: 2024945864

ISBN: 9781957832500 (pbk)
ISBN: 9781957832470 (epub)

This book is dedicated to Catherine Billings, who although she is no longer with us, remains in my mind and heart. Her memory inspired me to write this book, which allows me to share what a wonderful person and mother she was to her family, students, and children.

 "You can fool all of the people some of time; you can fool some of the people all of the time, but you can't fool all the people all the time."

—*attributed to Abraham Lincoln*

Contents

Foreword...ix

Introduction...xiii
    My newspaper article about my sister.................xiv

Chapter 1: How The Media Reports......................1
    What is the purpose of a free press in a democracy?....1
    Brainwashing and Dehumanization........................3

Chapter 2: How Yellow Journalism was Born in the US...6
    Relationships influence media bias.....................7

Chapter 3: How Do I Know What to Believe in the Media?....9
    Types of reasoning help determine truth...............10
    How media causes anger................................12

Chapter 4: How the Media, in Conjunction with the Government, Influences the Public....14
    Gaslighting...15
    Boiling Frog Syndrome.................................16
    The COVID-19 vaccine mass distribution is a prime example of how brainwashing, gaslighting, and boiled frog syndrome was applied in convincing the public to initially accept the COVID-19 vaccine...18

Chapter 5: How the Media and Government Controlled the Narrative on COVID-19 19
Denial can be hazardous to your mental and physical health 19

Chapter 6: How Does Fear Affect a Person? 23
The state of fear 24
Instructions for finding VAERS website 25

Chapter 7: Understanding Negative Projection or Transference as a Possible Reason for Hurtful Behavior 27

Chapter 8: The Loss of Freedom and Its Effects on Human Beings 31
Freedom-depriving practices defined 32
Choice theory psychology defined 34

Chapter 9: Khrushchev's Advice 35
How to create a Socialistic and Communist State 35
The Lawsuit 36

Chapter 10: The New Art of War 37
Should I Believe William J. Holstein's Book, *The New Art of War: China's Deep Strategy Inside the United States?* 37
How to create a Socialistic and Communist state 39

Chapter 11: Medicine Cures Diseases of the Body; Wisdom Liberates the Soul of Sufferings 41
Effects of brain-altering drugs 41

Chapter 12: The Media and Tribalism, is it Good or Bad? 44

Chapter 13: First, They Came! 47
The Triad in the US 47
Dr. Peter McCullough's approach 49

Chapter 14: You Can't Fool All of The People All of The Time . . . 54
Involvement lists 56

Chapter 15: Veteran Suicides and the Media 58

Chapter 16: The Media, Big Pharma, and Politicians 63
    Do the media, big pharma, and politicians truly report on actual
        causes of mass shootings?. 63
    A reasonable solution 63
    The Columbine killer 66

Chapter 17: The Homeless Problem 68
    The inhumane closure of mental hospitals 69

Chapter 18: How Does the Media Contribute to
Human Suffering? 71
    Who becomes a gang member? 73

Chapter 19: COVID-19 Vaccine Injury 75
    Information from DOD data 75
    January 26, 2022, *Covid Vaccines Causing Miscarriages, Cancer, and
        Neurological Disorders Among Military, DOD Data Show*. 75

About the Author 78

Foreword

In a world where many foundational concepts appear backward or upside down, Bart P. Billings, PhD, COL (Ret.), shines a spotlight on the corrupt media and brings needed transparency into a former sacred cow, where money, power, and political influence have ruled the day. Dr. Billings is no newcomer to battling forces that others dare not explore.

In this book, How the Media Creates Victims in Our Society, Dr. Billings investigates the role of the media and its use of brainwashing and coercive persuasion techniques to cause conformity and to gain compliance in the unsuspecting public sector. It is made shockingly clear, how the media has changed over the years, away from reporting the news to making the news.

I have been particularly impressed with Dr. Billings's characterization of systematic desensitization in his book, and how this lulls the public into a sense of complacency and obedience.

Instead of the media acting as the guard dogs for transparency and honesty, Dr. Billings progressively unravels their continuous attempts to readjust our realities through distortion

and reconfiguration of our perceptions. The media's artful technology can cause day to appear as night and right to appear as wrong. Even one's certainty of their own facts can be shot full of alleged contradictions until their facts reappear as fiction and their certainty is overwhelmed.

Dr. Billings provides an in-depth analysis of just how the media creates victims in our society. With his extensive knowledge and expertise, Dr. Billings reveals how violent college demonstrations that deprive students of their civil rights and ability to attend class are transformed into demonstrations where the rioters become the victims and the victims are labeled as criminals! And, when pressed, the actual rioters can't even answer why they are there!

As a veteran advocate, I have become involved with political and governmental issues.

My intention has been to help inform and protect others who have omitted or misguided information that could be detrimental to their health. So many veterans have chosen to commit suicide, while others are depressed or agitated, and others have even become homicidal. Over the years, in my conversations with many veterans, veterans service organizations, and caregivers, it has become very apparent that veterans do not know the side effects of medications they are being prescribed.

As Dr. Billings points out in his previous book, Invisible Scars, The Food and Drug Administration (FDA) has placed black box warning labels (indicating highest risk) on a number of medication classifications, including antidepressants, antipsychotics, benzodiazepines, stimulants, narcotics, and anxiolytics. And the first side effect listed on those medication warning labels is suicide ideation.

How can it be that the veteran suicide rate has remained about 6,000 per year for over 10 years?

How could that be? This seems contrary to the press reports and medical officials on veterans' issues. Adding even more confusion is when I attended a three-hour congressional hearing in Washington, DC on the issue of veteran suicides. It, surprisingly, did not highlight or question any information about the medications and their potential side effects, which the first listed is suicide. I should note that Dr. Billings, in the past, convinced Congress to hold hearings on the relationship between psychiatric medications and suicide among our veterans. This information and his testimony can also be found in his book, Invisible Scars.

This is common medical knowledge, yet there seems to be an apparent agreement or a mystery at best, to keep this information low profile, so it's less likely for veterans to understand.

My observations have led me to conclude that the media does not report on how the Government has been responsible for veteran suicides to continue for decades. It has avoided doing standard investigative reporting as to the real cause and potential solutions, such as informed consent on psychiatric medications.

It appears that the media's focus is more political and financial, at present. It is no secret that DC lobbyists have billions to influence Congress, but what effects are these billions having on the watchdogs of our vulnerable country?

I decided to dig further and actually read the section in the Veteran Administrative Handbook, chapter on "Informed Consent". I was shocked to learn that there is no way of proving that our veterans are being provided with informed consent, as the enforcement mechanism is verbal consent. It therefore can't be enforced. There is no accountability!

I worked with a US congressman who agreed this needed to be investigated. He engaged the Government Accountability Office to look into this. Part of the results in their report is that the Veterans Administration had no evidence that they have provided treatment options to their patients.

Some integrative treatment options (as identified in Dr. Billings' previously mentioned book, Invisible Scars) are chiropractic, yoga, acupuncture, canine and equine therapy, exercise therapy, cognitive behavioral therapy, art therapy, hyperbaric oxygen therapy, and other therapies. Treatment options and side effects are the two foundational points provided to a veteran which comprise informed consent.

So, where was the media blasting this revelation from shore to shore?
Nowhere to be found!! Sadly, the evidence of media manipulation appears as omnipresent, in so many aspects of our society. As a concerned citizen, my goal now is to get the Government to pass laws to implement informed consent.

Dr. Billings has shared with me, "People tell me that I saved their lives because they read my book." They say "It sounds like you were talking to me. I came to your conference. I had it all planned to commit suicide on Monday. I read your book over the weekend . . . You saved my life." Dr. Billings told me that his greatest failure in life is when he has failed to get Invisible Scars, to the desperate suicidal veterans. It acts like a tourniquet to committing suicide and needs to be applied.

It takes grit from someone like Dr. Billings to expose such instances and tie in the related evidence for all to see. This is where Dr. Billings's background and backbone shine through.

My hat is off to Dr. Billings, as he realizes these omissions by the media, and is stepping forward to protect his fellow veterans. When the government is not taking the needed responsibility to protect us and the media has fallen under the influence of vested interests, it is comforting to know that personal integrity lives in those who put it all on the line.

John Spagnola, *President/CEO, Veterans Strategic Solutions*

Introduction

I have been asked, "Does the media teach people destructive behavior?"
I don't want to paint the media with a broad brush, but would like to point out how various media outlets can have a serious negative impact on our society. Yes, there are factual and objective media sites, but for many years, in our country, the trend has been toward sensationalism, increasing ratings and profits, and sacrificing truthful and honest presentations. I was strongly impacted by this in a court case that I attended in Connecticut in the 80s.

In 1985, I started to write this book after observing firsthand how the corrupt media creates victims in our society.

At the time, I was attending a murder trial of a sibling, (story below that I wrote for Scranton Tribune) and then saw firsthand how the media glorifies criminals.

When the local newspaper, which was in a different state from the trial, asked my family if we would be willing to be interviewed, I asked, "Who would the story be about?" I was told it would be about the criminal's background and relationship with our family. I refused the interview and stated that if they wanted an interview about the victim of the crime, we would be willing to talk with them.

The following Sunday's supplemental magazine had a full front-page picture of the criminal, with a small postage-stamp-size picture of the victim at the very bottom. It was then that I realized the media was glorifying criminal behavior to sell newspapers and make as much money as possible (very much like William Randolph Hurst demonstrated in the early days of newspaper publishing).

When the story was initially presented in the community newspaper, the local small-town residents had the insight to see what was so obviously happening and many complained or canceled their local newspaper subscriptions. The newspaper re-contacted me because of the community reaction and asked me if I would write a story about the victim of the crime. I proceeded to write a three-day series about our sibling and the person she was to her family and community. It was then that I also realized that the media was primarily interested in making money and not concerned how destructive their stories could be to people in general.

My newspaper article about my sister

The following newspaper articles are released with thanks to The Times-Tribune, Scranton, PA. Scrantonian Tribune: by Bart P Billings, Ph.D.

December 20, 1987, First day

Slain Woman's Families Responds: "Manfredi; A Quest For Power"

Scrantonian Tribune
Serving Northeast Pennsylvania since 1856

SUNDAY, DECEMBER 20, 1987 — 25 cents

Slain woman's family responds:
Manfredi: A quest for power

By Dr. Bart P. Billings

SCRANTON — On March 8, 1985, Russell Manfredi hit his wife, Catherine, over the head repeatedly with a baseball bat in their bedroom. He proceeded to drop her from the second-story window, head-first, to the concrete below. He then placed her in the family car and drove several blocks and purposely crashed it into a pole. He returned home and tried to convince friends and family that Catherine drove off and got into a car accident. He was caught in his lie and went to trial one-and-one-half years later. He was out on bail most of the time. After about two months of trial he was convicted of first degree manslaughter and is now free walking the streets, waiting on his request for an appeal. The appeal process takes from one to one-and-one-half years before a decision will be made on whether or not it is granted.

The following is the first installment in a three-part series by Dr. Bart P. Billings, whose sister Catherine Billings Manfredi was murdered by her husband Russell Manfredi in 1985. The Scrantonian Tribune asked members of Cathy's family if they wanted to respond to the four-part series that was published last week in this newspaper. The following article is that statement. It was written shortly after the trial and conviction of Russell Manfredi.

In the family one and damn court to all of the above-mentioned actions. The people who live in the community called this trial, "The Man Who Killed His Wife Three Times."

Victims of crime, especially violent crime, are the most overlooked people in our society. When people say that this country has developed a throwaway attitude, this philosophy also extends to people. But nowhere is it seen more than in the families and friends of a victim of a violent crime – a victim who has had her life taken away from her and will never be able to return or reclaim this possession.

If you ask the dictionary you see several definitions of victim. One of the definitions reads as follows: "A living creature slain and offered as a sacrifice to a deity or as part of a religious rite." When you stop and think of how this definition pertains to our society, you develop an awareness of why victims are overlooked. Without the victims there would be no movies, sensational newspaper headlines or adrenalin-pumping TV news reports depicting murders, wars, sex abuse, substance

(Please turn to Page A15)

Manfredi's quest

(Continued from Page One)

(drugs and alcohol) abuse, fraud and on and on. The victims are, in fact, a sacrifice our society offers to the god of money, a religion followed by many people. Victimization results in many media organizations making big money when they advertise, through their coverage, all the different ways a person can be exploited. But it doesn't stop with these organizations making the big bucks. It goes to the opposite extreme of being a victim, to criminals who gain notoriety and financial rewards once their story is published and, at times, even made into a movie. It is not unheard of that these destroyers of life and other societal standards make more money from their stories than the winners of the Nobel Peace Prize.

The case which is always present with us is that at our sister Cathy, or Catherine Billings Manfredi as the papers call her, when a Hartford, Conn., newspaper printed an extensive magazine story, with a front-page picture of her killer, Russell Manfredi. The story focused totally on Russell Manfredi, with brief references to Cathy.

The reporter tried to make it look like Cathy's family was not willing to cooperate in providing information. What he did not state was that the family was not willing to sanction a story that was to focus on the criminal, poor Russell Manfredi. The family even offered the reporter an open invitation to discuss Cathy's life history if the story focused on the victim and her family's grief. This was refused. How else could those who benefit from the unfortunate's demise ascend to their castles, which are built on the bones of the victims they fail to acknowledge? It's hard to understand how the so-called leaders of our society fail to realize that their inattention to victims and the laws and publicity that benefit the criminal reinforce and expand victimization. But stop again and ask yourself – maybe they do know about this ritual; how can they not know that there are more disheveled people in our country who are not meeting their psychological needs, even in minimal ways?

One of the basic needs we all must meet is to be in control of our lives. Even if it is to a lesser degree, we all need to feel this need for power is being met. Our leaders meet this need most of the time just by being in leadership roles, others meet it by doing a good job at work or through other efforts that build self worth. Irresponsible people in our society, who have not learned to meet this need, suffer extreme pain every day of their lives, in an unfilled attempt to gain power. Thus comes the big story and hype on how to meet this need immediately, with little work: it's on the front page, on the radio, in the movies – every day, the ultimate power – to take a life, to kill someone. And the consequence, no matter how brief or long it lasts, is power. Examples that come to mind are mass killings, hostage holding, and killing innocent people, with all these acts getting press coverage and being in the spotlight for months, even years, while the lengthy legal process goes on and on. All the while questions about the criminal are being asked by the media to stimulate interest: why did he do it, was he insane at the time, did the victim cause it? Who has the answers? It becomes a media game show with the big winners being the publicists (TV, radio, papers, etc.) and the star – the criminal. No one stops to ask an elementary question, did his behavior (action) result in her death? This is too simple a question to answer, for the answer would result in a conclusion. Who wants a conclusion to stop this wild ride? Not the attorneys who prepare for theatre each day in court and await anxiously that evening for the media's review of their performance; not the expert witnesses who battle each other to see who is the more convincing and who has the most credentials; and most of all, not the media. For all, the worship of money supercedes justice – which is simply asking, who is responsible for this action?

Through all of this, one thing becomes clear – that is, how unclear things become, to the point of people forgetting who the victim really was, and how difficult life is for the remaining victims, i.e., the family and friends who have to witness this menagerie of confusion and contempt. Does one realize that the only people who really want a quick end to this travesty of injustice are the loved ones of the victim? The victim's pain ended with her death, but now, the criminal continues to inflict pain, with the help of the system, on those who have lost a part of themselves in the deceased.

The people who loved Cathy and who are members of a deeply hurt, loving family can never forget the long days in the courtroom. The theatrics of the attorneys and expert witnesses, the crowding and shoving media personnel in the small room in back of the courtroom, the charming, quaint chase the court stenographer had with the criminal during the breaks in full view of everyone. The chess game in the courtroom was so obvious that you start to wonder if it was real or just a bad dream. The accused, as he was called, sitting not at the table in front facing his accusers, but three rows back in the audience like a bystander. We were informed that this is permissible and that he only has to be in the courtroom. One starts to wonder if he realized he was being accused of murder. His friends and family surrounded and guarded him with their presence and looks of support, to the point of giving the impression; How dare the victim cause this inconvenience and grief upon us? If she didn't "choose" for herself to be brutally killed, they would not have to put up with all this publicity.

But wait a moment. Prior to this they were never quoted in the paper or on television. Is it all that bad? This attention can be contagious, but who could ever admit that, least of all the poor criminal and his family.

Even a priest wants a piece of the action. Like a puppet in black clothing, whose strings are controlled by the criminal and his eloquent, high-priced lawyer, he sits in the audience next to his demigod during the final days of trial. One wonders, does he realize what he is doing, how his presence can influence the jury to think that the Roman Catholic Church supports this killer? When asked these questions during a break, one can't believe he is not as aware of his actions as you would like a man of the cloth to be. When asked if he could dress in clothing other than his priestly garments, he flatly refused – even after he was told that the Bishop's secretary said he could. Then, asked if he knew the victim's family had the same religious beliefs as those of his parish, he appears confused, giving the impression it is more noble to save a soul instead of help the suffering. He comments to one family member that the accused told him he didn't think it would be a good idea to talk to Cathy's family. But again, there is more press, being at the side of the accused. He is in full view in the courtroom, not doing the work of his church in private, away form the lights and notoriety of the royal court, where the teachings of his church say it should be done. You cannot help to think that this priest may be so caught up in this whirlwind of power, he is now worshipping the wrong god.

The major theme of the trial always goes back to the premise that Dr. Manfredi is not responsible for his behavior and had no choice but to kill his wife. How could a man called "doctor" do such a thing? The word doctor is used over and over as if to try to instill in everyone present the thought that this person is special and above such a thing as murder. Why else would they call him "doctor"? This is not a hospital setting or a medical office where the title connotes patient-physician services. But this is a courtroom, where the title "mister" is the standard measure of who one is. But not once was Russell Manfredi referred to as a "mister."

Tomorrow: The trial continues.

December 21, 1987
 "Manfredi had no remorse"
Victim's Family Recalls Manfredi Trial

Scrantonian Tribune

Serving Northeast Pennsylvania since 1856

MONDAY, DECEMBER 21, 1987 — 25 cents

Murder victim's kin:
Manfredi had no remorse

This is the second part of a three-part series written by Dr. Bart P. Billings, brother of Catherine Billings Manfredi, who was murdered in 1985 by Russell Manfredi, her husband. The Scrantonian Tribune published a four-part series last week on Russell Manfredi and the newspaper requested from Cathy's family any statement that they wished to make on the case.

By Dr. Bart P. Billings

The major theme of (Russell Manfredi's murder) trial always went back to the premise that Dr. Manfredi is not responsible for his behavior and had no choice but to kill his wife. How could a man called "doctor" do such a thing? The word doctor is used over and over as it to try to instill in everyone present the thought that this person is special and above such a thing as murder. Why else would they call him "doctor"? This is not a hospital setting or a medical office where the title connotes patient-physician services. But this is a courtroom where the title "mister" is the standard measure of who one is; not once was Russell Manfredi referred to as a "mister".

There is never a time throughout the trial where Cathy can defend herself against the innuendoes offered up by the defense, which tries to depict her as something less than what she really was — a caring, vibrant and loving mother and wife. If she did have a fault, it was caring too much. But the defense strategically tries to position Cathy in a light that would condone killing her by trying to indirectly imply she abused her children and that is the reason for the quarrel that led to her death. Although there is not one shred of evidence of this even being close to the truth, this is their only defense to get away with murder. One almost expects the defendant to accuse his wife of husband abuse, dramatically ripping off his shirt and revealing scars, but this may be a little too much, even for the defense attorney to pull off. These maneuvers require a great deal of skill by the defense attorney, for one mistake can cause a backlash. This is, I believe, the excitement which drives the defense attorney and gives him many hours of discussion with colleagues over drinks. If successful at developing this slanderous smokescreen without being overtly detected by a less skilled prosecution attorney, his financial value increases in the market place.

The thought strikes me that

(Please turn to Page 11)

Victim's family recalls

(Continued from Page One)

Mark Twain was correct when he said, "The only native American criminal is a lawyer." For now I can see clearly that king money is primary and if justice happens on the way to making a dollar, it's coincidental. This idea got further reinforced one day at lunch, while the trial was in progress. We were at a restaurant with two attorneys who were assisting our family. We were joined by a friend of theirs who was an extremely well-known attorney, who seldom, if ever, lost a case. As we talked and he began to see our frustration with the system, tried to help us understand why the verdicts handed down have little to do with what is logically correct. He made it clear that our system is not fair and effective as people are led to believe, but that the results of a trial, for the most part, really depend on who has the best attorney. This fact was so evident in the Manfredi trial that at one time, during a recess, I approached the prosecution attorney and asked him who was running the courtroom, the defense attorney or the judge? It was extremely evident to all that the defense attorney was disqualifying a hostile witness who is very obviously jealous of Cathy, even in death. This small person, both in stature and character, obviously was here to meet her needs for power and worth, which hopefully can be accomplished through the attention of the media and press. She is completely devastated when not allowed to make this grandstand appearance and the anger in her face for the deprivation betrays her motive to be supposedly help, but in the long run, her being allowed to testify could have benefited the case against Manfredi, for her contempt for Cathy would have been obvious to everyone and her testimony rendered valid, casting doubt on the quality of witnesses brought forth by the defense. Even when the defense gets their witness to discuss Cathy, they stand firm in stating Cathy was a good mother and wife, contrary to what the defense attorney is trying to lead them to state.

But the most devastating part of the trial to the living victims are the pictures of the body. These pictures cover all aspects of Cathy's death, from the initial death scene to the autopsy report showing the side of her skull with her brain removed. Many family members took away but even an inadvertent glance at the slides on a large screen will result in nightmares for the rest of their lives. How could such a brutal killing be treated so lightly, especially after seeing those pictures? How can he sit there never saying he was sorry and not showing remorse? If the family of the victim can see this and control their rage and not go after Manfredi in the courtroom, how can he say that he became angry enough that had to bludgeon his wife to death? The answer appears obvious to the living victims; he chose his behavior, which was to kill his wife. It all boils down to the final curtain call. The closing dramatic remarks to the jury by the attorneys, the instructions to the jury by the judge and the long several days waiting for the verdict.

The rumors fly. We hear that 11 of the 12 jurors want first-degree murder. Maybe there will be justice, but we are told to remember that it must be unanimous to get first-degree murder. This means that the defense attorney only has to convince one person that his client was too emotionally upset to be responsible for the killing. The odds are in favor of this happening, for there has to be one bleeding heart who wants to forgive and forget. We have previously seen this behavior in the courtroom in the presence of the priest.

Tomorrow: The verdict; Who was Catherine Billings Manfredi?

December 22, 1987

Slain Woman's Brother's Recalls:

"Cathy was a loving and devoted mother"

I started to do some research after this experience and one of my many findings revealed what the general values of people, who were in various aspects of the media, were at that time.

In the 1980s, when values discussions were in vogue, I reviewed a study, where a researcher surveyed the values of people in various aspects of the media. What was discovered was those producers, writers, editors, etc., had quite different values than the general population. At the time, the study showed only about 7% of them had any religious values, 9% believed that a person should be married one time and be faithful to their partner, etc., etc. The result of the survey revealed that, not only did people in the media have quite contrasting values from the general population, but felt their responsibility was to impose their values on the rest of society.

In a later study published in USA Today, it was revealed that the media was moving their work in the direction of the values they expressed in the 80s survey. Examples i.e., TV shows like *Ozzie and Harriot* and *Father Knows Best* became *Three's Company, Modern Family*, etc. From news reporters who write the facts of a story to ones that practice yellow journalism to sell papers. The saying, "never let the truth get in the way of a good story," has never been so prevalent as it is today. Journalism has moved from reporting facts to becoming another form of entertainment.

Over the years, I have seen the general goals of people in the media come to fruition in movies, television, newspaper articles and now social media. It's up to everyday people, like the ones I described in the small eastern town above, to decide and choose to state, if they desire, that enough is enough and express their own values with the money they refuse to spend on distorted and hurtful media.

So, the answer to the main question above is YES, the media can and does influence human behavior.

One of my most vivid experiences of this is when I interviewed gang members who participated in a drive-by shooting, telling me that even though they were not identified in a newspaper article describing the shooting, they carried the article in their wallets to show their friends what they did. Words in the article, i.e., they were cunning and eluded the police glorified their acts. If words describing their criminal behavior, i.e., they were cowards terrified of being identified, it is doubtful they would carry this article in their wallets.

It's also not unusual for mentally defective people (many on black box warning, brain-altering psychiatric medications, with some side effects; suicide, homicide, depression, etc. . . . and/or illegal drugs) to become mass shooters, wanting the notoriety they learned other shooters have received from the media. In the past, the media usually showed their crimes and faces for days. Recently, public pressure has convinced some media not to show them.

However, when the criminals are shown on TV and in newspapers, it results in other potential villains wanting their similar 15 minutes, days, or weeks of glory, even if they are killed at the end of the story.

Also, it is not unusual for individuals to recreate movie or TV scenes resulting in violence or tragedy. I remember a movie scene where an individual was dodging cars on a busy freeway. I mentioned to my wife that there would be a similar act within a week on one of our streets. One week later, a teenager was reported killed in a similar act.

"Knowledge is power." (Francis Bacon, Meditationes Sacrae, 1597)

Chapter 1

How The Media Reports

What is the purpose of a free press in a democracy?

This is a question that was asked in an ability test I often administered. Today the answer to that question would not be correct if answered the way the test intended it to be answered. What has been occurring in the past decade is that the media, for the most part, has taken political sides and slants the news subjectively to one side or the other. Just presenting the objective facts is not the focus as it was intended to be when our country was created. We can see the roots of the media, when we go back 5,000 years, when Scribes were trained to report activities in ancient Egypt.

An article titled, "Sacred animals of ancient Egypt", states Thoth was the god of writing and knowledge in ancient Egypt. Thoth was also the god of the moon, sacred texts, mathematics, the sciences, magic, messenger and recorder of the deities, master of knowledge, and patron of scribes. His Egyptian name was Djehuty, which means "He who is like the Ibis." He was depicted as an ibis bird or a baboon.

In the Bible, Thoth is a very high-ranking and important demon. He is one of the seven sons of Satan. He is the most brilliant and intellectual of the Gods. He is very likable, extremely charismatic, and friendly. This leads me to the question, who is the God the present media members of untruths worship?

1

Chapter 1

It is interesting to read the following Bible verses and think of the current-day media as the scribes and the current-day politicians as the Pharisees.

Jesus spoke to the crowds and to his disciples, saying, "The scribes and the Pharisees have taken their seat on the chair of Moses. Therefore, do and observe all things whatsoever they tell you, but do not follow their example. For they preach but they do not practice" (Matthew 23:1–3 New American Bible Revised Edition).

Most often, children of scribes in ancient Egypt became scribes. Although some commoners were able to get their sons into the school for scribes, it was very rare. Today where do the current media people come from? It appears to be a closed society, just as it was in ancient Egypt.

Today's media readily demonstrates their innate values openly, by what they write and produce. A sample of this can be observed in a survey done years ago.

In 1986, an article, based on a survey, was written by Linda S Lichter, S Robert Lichter and Stanley Rothman titled, "Hollywood and America: The Odd Couple." The article appeared in the Tocqueville Review of the University of Toronto.

The initial statement in their journal article stated, "Conservatives and liberals harmonize on few issues, but they are, at least, equally vehement in criticizing television entertainment. On the liberal side, women and minority groups claim that television's unflattering portrayals of them perpetuate negative stereotypes. Conservatives object to the loose morality which they view as undermining the traditional American values of family, hard work, and patriotism. And myriad groups, from the PTA to the National Institute of Mental Health, worry that pervasive television violence is breeding aggressive individuals and even criminals."

Their initial statement was consistent with my observations then and now.

The authors of this study state that they interviewed 104 of Hollywood's influential television writers, producers, and executives as part of a larger study of elite groups. There were approximately 350 names from which they sampled randomly. Of 172 individuals who were contacted, 104 agreed to be interviewed. They found that many of the media people were raised in big cities on the East and West Coast and very few had their roots in Middle America. This goes back to what took place in ancient Egypt, where scribes were mostly from an elite group and not the commoners. When dealing with religious upbringing, this study found that most of the people they interviewed were more secular in their orientation. Although 93% had religious upbringing, 93% said they seldom or never attend religious services. What was very interesting was that 75% of the people interviewed saw themselves as left of center politically, compared to only 14% who placed themselves to the right of center.

When it came to marriage, only 17% agreed that extramarital affairs were wrong. What was interesting was that most people in the media who were interviewed felt it was their obligation to impose their values on the rest of the American society. It was their social liberalism that most clearly distinguished them from the public. They clearly stated they were not in their profession primarily for the money, but they sought to move their audiences toward their own values for the good of society.

Although this survey was done almost 40 years ago, it still reflects even more so what we are seeing now in the people working in the US media.

Brainwashing and Dehumanization

I will never forget what a long-time journalist once told me. The first day in her first journalism class her professor told the class it was their duty to not just report the news, but to influence the public in their beliefs.

Today, this is more prevalent than ever in how most of the media reports and does not report the news. In the 1986 study, it was revealed that 75% of the media was politically left of center. Today, this figure may be much higher based on how the media supports left-leaning agendas. It is a difficult task to follow the principle that the purpose of a free press is to report on the government to keep it honest, if most of the media is, in fact, part of a political party. A 2024 example of this skewed reporting was the general media's lack of reporting of the US President's neurological problems over the previous four years. It took a 90-minute presidential debate to show the citizens of the country that their president was having cognitive problems when answering questions. It did not take a clinical psychologist to make this determination. Finally, some of the left-of-center press suggested that the president should not continue in his position or run for re-election. The problem was that some politicians and press ignored these obvious facts for their own benefit. What we have here not only echoes the title of this book, *How the Media Creates Victims in Our Society*, but expands it to *How the Media Can Victimize the United States of America by not honestly reporting on a Commander-in-Chief who has observable cognitive problems*. Being a retired military officer, if this were the case in the military, the officer with the observable cognitive problems would be replaced and sent for treatment.

I was involved in a similar situation when I was a Captain in the Army Reserve. I encountered a Colonel Psychiatrist who was not competent and actually creating significant problems for other staff and patients. I confronted him in the presence of my commanding officer and requested he be removed. Within one month, he was removed from his position and retired, and our program continued without him.

Chapter 1

    As dangerous as this situation is, on July 13, 2024, we saw an even more dangerous aspect of what the media has created in the United States. That was the attempted assassination of former president and potential presidential candidate, Donald Trump. For years, the media has been extremely negative in reporting on a person they oppose politically to the point of heavily influencing sociopathic-leaning individuals to attempt an assassination. Very similar to the attempted murderers of the congressman on a baseball field in DC several years ago. The constant brainwashing and dehumanization regarding political opponents, comparing them to Hitler and pure evil, leads to extreme hate and potential violence, which I will describe in detail later in this book.

    Now, I want to elaborate on dehumanization, since it appears to be weaponized as a political tool to figuratively and literally destroy an opponent. Oxford Languages defines dehumanization as "the process of depriving a person or group of positive human qualities.

    I experienced this personally when I was with a gathering of people at an event. Since people were talking about the recent assassination attempt, a person who I had known previously blurted out, "Too bad he wasn't killed!" Since he was standing behind where I was sitting, I immediately stood up and faced him, letting him know that his comment was inappropriate and reflected the type of behavior that takes place in a third-world country. I explained that I served in the military so people could be free to express their opinions without fear of being killed. This person quickly changed his comment, stating that he just meant that Trump should not be able to run for president.

    Primarily wishing for someone to be killed is one effect of politically weaponizing dehumanization. One can see it was used successfully, as a media weapon, by all sides during World War II. The purpose was to reduce the enemy to being less than human, thus lowering any inhibition a person may have to destroy them by any means possible.

Chapter 2

How Yellow Journalism was Born in the US

So, what is Yellow Journalism?
Yellow journalism was, and is, a style of newspaper reporting, as well as television, that emphasizes sensationalism over facts.

A classic example, during its heyday in the late 19th century, was one of many factors that helped push the United States and Spain into war in Cuba.

William Randolph Hearst owned a newspaper that played a huge part in arousing the public's intention to go to war with Spain. This activity reached its zenith after running several years of articles concerning the situation in Cuba, Hearst ran a series of articles blaming the Spanish for the sinking of the *Maine* with a mine. For years, many people in the United States blamed Spain for starting the war. But in 1976, a team of American naval investigators concluded that the *Maine* explosion was likely caused by a fire that ignited its ammunition stocks, not by a Spanish mine or act of sabotage.

The Spanish-American War is often referred to as the first "media war." During the 1890s, journalism that sensationalized — and **sometimes even manufactured** (as occurs often today) — dramatic events was a powerful force that helped propel the United States into war with Spain, resulting in many people becoming victims of the media. The relationship between Spain and the US became so strained, they could no longer discuss the situation. By April 21, 1898, the Spanish-American War had begun, resulting in two major countries being victimized by the media.

This war resulted in 2,446 American deaths from various causes, as well the deaths of almost 16,000 Spanish soldiers. After this war, Spain never regained its status as a world power, as it was prior to the war. In a sense, the media affected a whole country's status as a world leader.

William Randolph Hearst, (born April 29, 1863, San Francisco, California, US, died August 14, 1951, Beverly Hills, California), was an American newspaper publisher who built up the nation's largest newspaper chain and whose methods profoundly influenced American journalism. The Hearst family is the 23rd wealthiest family in the world, with a combined $24.5 billion net worth.

Hearst, in a sense, built his castle in California on the bones of the victims he created with his yellow journalism.

Relationships influence media bias

Why are so many media outlets providing similar biased information?

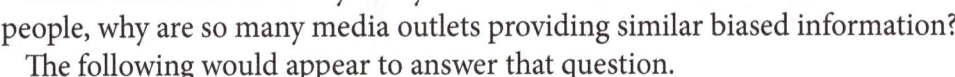

I have often been asked by many people, why are so many media outlets providing similar biased information?

The following would appear to answer that question.

Most of the people listed below have values not generally consistent with the general population in the US. The survey I mentioned in Chapter 1 shows that people in the media's values were drastically different from the general population. The summary of the survey stated that, although the media had very different values than the general population in the US, they felt a duty to impose their values on the rest of society through their profession. Almost 40 years later, we can see that they are achieving their stated goals through inner relationships with people in power.

Some of the involvements with the people below show how relationships with each other, are consistent with how they have accomplished meeting their inherent values, which generally are contrary, not only to most of America but also contrary to Natural Laws for Human Existence.

Over the past 25 to 30 years, it appears the news has been spoon-fed to the masses, based on the values of a select few.

It becomes a little clearer now, from prior information, on how people are involved through various types of relationships. What follows is a small sample of influential people and their relationships.

- The Governor of Michigan used to work for George Soros.
- Calif Gov. Gavin Newsome is Nancy Pelosi's nephew.
- Congressman Adam Shiff's sister is married to George Soros's son.
- John Kerry's daughter is married to a Mullah's son in Iran.

- Hillary's daughter, Chelsea, is married to George Soros's nephew.
- ABC News executive producer Ian Cameron is married to Susan Rice, Obama's former National Security Adviser.
- CBS President David Rhodes is the brother of Ben Rhodes, Obama's Deputy National Security Adviser for Strategic Communications.
- ABC News correspondent Claire Shipman is married to Jay Carney, former Obama White House Press Secretary.
- ABC News and Univision reporter Matthew Jaffe is married to Katie Hogan, Obama's former Deputy Press Secretary.

This is what you call a "stacked deck."

If you had a hunch the news system was somewhat rigged and you couldn't put your finger on it, this might help you expose the puzzle. This is huge, and is only a 'partial' list since the same relationships hold true for most media outlets.

That's why many people think there might be a bias in the news.

"The traditional research perspective is to caution about this type of interaction from a democratic perspective. If opinions and values of the citizens on policies, politicians, and institutions can be easily manipulated by elites, that can threaten democracy," says Karl Magnus Johansson, Professor of Political Science at Souderton University.

Chapter 3

How Do I Know What to Believe in the Media?

The latest and one of the most frequent questions I have been asked by people is, how do I know what to believe in media? There is no one answer other than spend all day watching various news channels on TV, reading newspapers and journals, and then conclude what may be true. A friend of mine does this but is still not sure what the truth is. Very few have this kind of time or skill, so there is no real answer to ensure what you are being told is true. It's like a crap shoot in the end.

There was a question on a Standardized Intelligent Test, which I gave years ago when I was seeing patients. It asked about the importance of a free press in a democracy. The answer expected, which would be correct, was to basically keep the government honest. But this question cannot have the same correct answer today. The reason is that the question would have to be changed to: Why is a free and HONEST press important in a democracy? The fact remains that there is no one keeping a free press honest in our current democracy. So, if the checks and balances of a press are nonexistent, what eventually happens to the government is that it becomes dishonest. The people in the democracy then don't know what is true, and they cannot cast a knowledgeable vote. This is the reason there need to be checks and balances to monitor a free press and ensure its honesty and truthfulness. Fake news must not be tolerated.

This is why there must be rules and guidelines governing the media itself, a MEDIA CONSTITUTION, with enforced laws and consequences for dishonest behavior that are more than mere retractions.

We should develop a licensing board, like we have in our medical and psychology communities. Media professionals should have requirements like honesty, due diligence, and other reporting standards when writing for publication. These standards can be monitored and reported on by both the public and other licensed media professionals, to ensure a reporter or news organization does not violate professional standards. If they violate reporting criteria and guidelines, their credentials could be temporarily removed and they would receive supervision or else seek other employment, depending on the board's mandates. Serious violations would lead to more stringent consequences.

Can one imagine a physician making a life-threatening error due to incompetence and just being asked to make a retraction stating they are sorry? In many ways, reporters can drastically affect a person's life by falsely reporting an occurrence and getting away with it by simply writing a retraction, which may not even be seen by the public. It's time a bright light is shined on the current corruption that is occurring in our media. That goes beyond filing a civil suit, which puts the burden back on the victim the media created.

A final thought on how do you know if people or the media are telling the truth?

Types of reasoning help determine truth

The University of Scranton is a Jesuit college in Pennsylvania which, when I attended, required its students to basically minor in philosophy. At the time, many of us complained about having to take all these classes, since we didn't immediately see how they would help us get a job when we graduated. But as the years passed, I came to see the value of the lessons they drilled us on.

Today, more than ever, I value the lessons learned in our philosophy classes about inductive and deductive reasoning, when evaluating what is true information and what is false information.

This website best explains the various ways of reasoning. (https://www.livescience.com/21569-deduction-vs-induction.html)

Deductive reasoning starts out with a general statement and examines the possibilities to reach a specific, logical conclusion. We go from the general to the specific observations.

An example of a false statement using deductive reasoning is: If the generalization is wrong, the resulting conclusion may be logical, but it may also be untrue. For example, the argument, "All bald men are grandfathers. Harold is bald. Therefore, Harold is a grandfather," is valid logically, but it is untrue because the original statement is false.

Inductive reasoning makes broad generalizations from specific observations. Basically, there is data, and then conclusions are drawn from the data. In inductive inference, we go from the specific to the general.

Even if all the premises are true in a statement, inductive reasoning allows for the conclusion to be false. Here's an example: "Harold is a grandfather. Harold is bald. Therefore, all grandfathers are bald." The conclusion does not follow logically from the statements.

Most people, when listening to media news, often use another form of reasoning, called **abductive reasoning**. This usually starts with an incomplete set of observations and proceeds to the likeliest possible explanation for the set of observations. It often entails making an educated guess after observing a phenomenon for which there is no clear explanation.

This type of reasoning is heavily dependent on a person's life experiences and education, more than Deductive or Inductive reasoning.

What I have always explained to my patients is that no two people can see anything 100% the same way, since we all have unique brains, the same as we have unique individual fingerprints. Therefore, most likely, we practice abductive reasoning.

It's important to understand that every conversation with another person is a disagreement, to various degrees. We must learn that people are right for themselves, based on their having unique brains. Since we are both right for ourselves, we must learn to compromise and negotiate to meet somewhere in the middle and retain some of our unique perceptions.

There are some instances when two people, or the media we observe, are so far apart in how things are viewed that there is no way we can meet anywhere near the center. For example, if I have a baseball team that is in California and you have one in New York, meeting halfway to play would require traveling too far. But if my team is in San Diego, California and yours is in Los Angeles, meeting halfway is reasonable. Therefore, we must remember that there are some people, or media outlets, that we can't deal with since we would have to go too far and give up too much of our beliefs to perceive.

If people can understand that each perception with another person, or the news media analyst, is a disagreement, to a degree, and that they are right for themselves, as we are for ourselves, then we can agree to disagree.

But if they, or we, only feel we are right for ourselves and the other person or media source is wrong, then we have an argument. An argument becomes emotional because we are trying to deprive another of their freedom to perceive. People will fight to the end to retain their freedom to perceive, since it is a basic human psychological need.

By using abductive, inductive, or deductive reasoning and understanding the difference between a disagreement and argument, we can come to understand more clearly what is true for ourselves and what media outlets and people we want to patronize.

Types of intellectual reasoning

One final thought on intellectual reasoning that I think is a critical thinking skill, is one's ability to have analogical thinking skills. As described in *Business* by Gennaro Cuofano, December 19, 2023:

"Analogical thinking is a cognitive process that involves recognizing similarities and making connections between seemingly unrelated concepts, situations, or problems. It is a fundamental aspect of human cognition and creativity, allowing individuals to draw on their knowledge and experiences to solve new problems, make predictions, and generate innovative ideas."

When I applied to graduate school, I was required to pass an analogical thinking test. At the time, I thought it was just another test, but as time went on, I saw the true value of this test and the wisdom of the program director, who required this test. Over my career, I have learned that one's ability to have strong analogical thinking skills is critical to success in all types of decision-making.

How media causes anger

Recognizing how the media might influence you to become angry, as mentioned above, makes it very difficult to determine what is factual news. Therefore, it is important for one to learn how the media's influence creates such strong beliefs that their presentations lead to angry conflicts with others.

Many people have asked me, "Why are there so many angry people currently, influenced by the media, who are exceptionally difficult to communicate with in a reasonable manner regarding current affairs?" The answer is a basic psychological concept, as well as a physiological premise.

Reciprocal inhibition is a psychological term, as well as a physiological term, which means you can't have two opposite emotions, or physical reactions, occurring at the same time, i.e., happy/depressed. It should be noted that this reaction can be heavily influenced by fear, since as I will later explain how fear causes physiological reactions that interfere with thinking clearly. For over 50 years, I have used this knowledge in my therapy sessions. I explain that if a person is angry/hateful based on false information, then they can't be calm/logical/reasonable at the same time. For example, this is the basis for Trump Derangement Syndrome, which is very real in many people. In this time of crisis, people still have too much hate generated by the media information to see straight. Just mentioning a contrary opinion will set people off into anger.

I have suggested not to talk to people who are often angry, who can't calmly listen to an opposite opinion, and who don't contribute to your happiness. Choose happiness in the people and media you expose yourself to! In these dire times, look for the positive. As I have told my patients over my career as a psychologist, "For every bad thing that happens (no matter how bad) to what you experience and hear, if you look hard enough, you will find two good things." If you can't—get someone to help you look for them.

What goes along with reciprocal inhibition is the Theory of Cognitive Dissonance (Leon Festinger, 1957). Festinger proposed that human beings strive for internal psychological consistency to enable them to mentally function in the real world.

An individual's "internal world" is a combination, primarily, of what they have experienced and learned throughout their life, which can be heavily influenced by the media. The perceptions they retain in their "real world" are the experiences and education that meet their basic and higher-level psychological needs (choice theory psychology principle), at that time in their life.

Since no two people have the exact same brain, nor the same education and experiences in life, it is therefore impossible for any two people to see the world 100 percent in the same way. As a result, to a certain degree, every conversation, as previously mentioned, is a disagreement. This varies to a lesser or greater degree based on their lifetime perceptions. That is why some people can disagree to a moderate degree and some to an extreme degree resulting in anger. This can trigger extreme cognitive dissonance that results in intense arguments, where one or both people try to get the other to believe their perceptions. These clashes result in one person trying to get the other to give up their freedom to perceive some of their media influences, lifetime values, and moral positions.

Therefore, when a person experiences internal inconsistency, they tend to become psychologically uncomfortable (cognitive dissonance) and are often motivated to reduce the cognitive dissonance. They tend to make changes to justify their stressful behavior, either by adding new parts to their cognition, which is causing the psychological dissonance, or by avoiding circumstances and contradictory information, which is likely to increase the magnitude of their cognitive dissonance.

For many people, coping with the nuances of contradictory ideas or experiences is mentally stressful. It requires energy and effort to sit with people whose opposing beliefs seem true to them. Festinger argued that some people would inevitably resolve dissonance by blindly believing whatever they wanted to believe, in spite of prevailing general realities.

"The pen is mightier than the sword." (Edward Bulwer-Lytton, *Richelieu; Or the Conspiracy*, 1839)

Chapter 4

How the Media, in Conjunction with the Government, Influences the Public

US President Abraham Lincoln allegedly once said, "You can fool all people some of the time and some people all the time. But you can never fool all people all the time."

Brainwashing may be looked at to somewhat answer the question; how can people's judgment be so clouded when they can't separate facts from mistruths?

In our current society, we moved beyond the past phenomenon, which was known as *subliminal perception*. This was when a person couldn't discriminate visual stimuli they report not consciously seeing. I remember being told about the movies showing popcorn so quickly that the image could not be consciously seen, but people would experience a craving for popcorn.

Brainwashing or coercive persuasion, more commonly called clouded judgement, is when people can't separate facts from mistruths.

Indirect hypnosis: In 1985, I was attending a murder trial and observed the expert witness psychiatrist testifying for the defendant. For a half hour, he was asked questions by the district attorney and then further questions by the defending attorney. I noticed that he was not interrupted one time by the prosecution with an objection. This was very unusual, since the psychiatrist was offering obvious misinformation, which was apparent to many people attending the trial.

What I observed as a reason for no prosecution objections was the fact that the expert witness was practicing indirect hypnosis. He was repeating the same information over and over in a monotone voice, while rocking slowly back and forth. The prosecutors were lulled into a state of compliance similar to what I experienced at times in a college classroom, when the professor, in a similar monotonous tone, lulls the class close to sleep.

When there was a recess in the trial, I had an opportunity to meet with the prosecutors and ask why they didn't object to the psychiatrist's testimony. They immediately realized that they didn't and appeared to be puzzled. When I explained that the witness was practicing indirect hypnosis, they responded, "What is that?" This was one of my first experiences where I was able to see a technique by which people's judgment can become so clouded they can't separate facts from mistruths.

Recently, I spoke with a professional high-powered lobbyist who spends much time in Washington, DC talking with various politicians. His job is to convince them to vote for policies that would benefit his company. He explained to me that big pharma alone spends in the vicinity of 900 million dollars for grassroots direct and indirect lobbying. To substantiate any company's spending on lobbying cost, one only needs to go to 990 IRS Search and click on the area, pharma, to get exact spending. Any type of company can be found here.

Also explained were various techniques to persuade people to think the way the agent desires. For example, we have all experienced how certain items pop up on our computer once we make an initial search. This is only the beginning. Lobbyists can go as far as sending information to someone they want to influence on Facebook, Instagram, and various other computer services. They can place signs on the road on your way to work. They can plant their agents in stores where you normally shop, to coincidentally talk with you and subsequently influence you. As good as the US lobbyists are, imagine how good the Chinese and Russians are in influencing whole countries.

The above example can be seen as forms of coercive persuasion or brainwashing. There are many ways to brainwash the public, with gaslighting being one.

Gaslighting

According to the *DSM–5*, the *Diagnostic and Statistical Manual of Mental Health* . . . we can see symptoms of depression, illnesses of the mind, that are caused by abuse, isolation, and/or *gaslighting*.

Gaslighting is a real psychological term discussed in literature. It's when reality changes over a long period of time, so slowly that it is not noticeable until a much later time. It is Communist China's preferred choice to take over other countries — like the US. The term comes from a play written in the 1930s, when the husband turned the gas lights lower each night for an extended period of time. When the wife asked, on occasion, if the light in the room was dim, the husband said no and ignored the question. When it got so dim in the room, the wife felt she was losing her mind, her husband told her the light was just fine.

I decided to mention gaslighting since my daughter experienced this psychological reaction in the past, although it was for a shorter period of time.

My daughter was driving home from work on a major LA highway at 6 p.m., when the police blocked the road and forced her off the highway. She had no choice but to obey the police, trusting the police directions would be fine, and did not have an option of which road to take as a detour. It wound up being an area in LA prone to violence in the past. She then was stopped by the same demonstrators that shut the highway down that she had to leave. People got in front of her car and were putting their hands on it. She was fearful for her life for the first time ever. She asked herself, why did the police force me to leave the highway and not ask the demonstrators to leave the highway? Her question to herself was, "Am I in the USA?" The next question was, why are peaceful people, simply driving on a highway, treated with so much disregard for their safety, when people who are illegally closing a highway are allowed to commit this unsafe act? The explanation she got was, they have the right to demonstrate. She asked herself, "Am I crazy?" *No, you are being gaslighted!*

Boiling Frog Syndrome

The boiling frog syndrome is similar to gaslighting since it applies to situations where one does not notice a change until it is too late. The theory was that to cook a frog, you put them in a pot of cold water and slowly heat it up. The frog, in reality, would jump out, but for years, this has been used as an analogy for slowly lulling people into acceptance of a policy.

Over the past year, I have seen the boiling frog syndrome, gaslighting, and brainwashing in action with the COVID-19 vaccine. I had the opportunity to talk to medical staff at three different hospitals, Imaging Centers, etc. Most of the people I spoke with were nurses, therapists, and technicians. Most had to get the COVID-19 vaccination shot to remain employed. Many did not get the booster shots since they started having new health problems occurring after the first vaccine shot. These were not older people, but people in the prime of their lives. Their honesty and willingness to talk to me in the privacy of a patient's hospital room and at their facility was a surprise, both in what they were saying and the length of time they spent talking. It appeared that they had found a person who was willing to listen to their concerns and would not chastise them. Their experience reminded me of the *boiling frog*.

In other words:

Below are both sides of the COVID-19 vaccine issue. You decide what is true or not for yourself.

Is there evidence available to corroborate the numbers of people who died or were injured from the COVID-19 vaccines? Yes, there most certainly is! Former Blackrock Fund Manager, Edward Dowd, was one of the first to sound the alarm about the massive increase in payouts for life insurance and health insurance benefits in February of 2022.

Also reported was a 163% increase in death benefits paid out for group life insurance policies by the 5th largest life insurance company in the US in 2021.

Official Government Data Record: 74,783 Deaths and 5,830,235 Injuries Following COVID-19 Vaccines in the US and Europe

June 25, 2022, 7:12 pm

Sophia Media, LLC, Vaccine Impact News

201 Hunters Crossing Blvd. Suite 10–149 Bastrop, TX 78602 USA

The European Medicines Agency (EMA) database of adverse drug reactions in 2022 has reported 45,752 deaths and 4,522,307 injuries following COVID-19 vaccines, while the United States vaccine's adverse events recording system in 2022 (VAERS) had reported 29,031 deaths and 1,307,928 injuries following COVID-19 vaccines.

We know that as huge as these numbers are, which are official government statistics, that they only represent a very small fraction of the total number of deaths and injuries suffered by those who chose (or were forced, e.g., active US military) to receive COVID-19 vaccines during the initial 18 months. In 2021, Dr. Jessica Rose did a comprehensive analysis to determine the "under-reported factor" in VAERS, and came up with 41X, meaning that the recorded data for adverse reactions to COVID-19 vaccines in VAERS had to be multiplied by 41 to get more accurate numbers. However, now that more time has elapsed since this study was performed, many feel that 41X is significantly too low, and should be closer to 100X, which is the number that was previously used based on a 2011 report by Harvard Pilgrim Health Care, Inc. for the US Department of Health, and Human Services (HHS). So, if we take the numbers available data from VAERS and the European EMA and multiply by 100, these would be the true numbers of adverse events following COVID-19 vaccines: 7,478,300 deaths and 583,023,500 injuries in Europe and the US.

The numbers are more than just figures on a paper. They are real people who were or presently are mothers, fathers, children, aunts, uncles, etc. . . .

It's a real crime against humanity.

The COVID-19 vaccine mass distribution is a prime example of how brainwashing, gaslighting, and boiled frog syndrome was applied in convincing the public to initially accept the COVID-19 vaccine.

To summarize the above, **propaganda** is the main word for much of what I have described.

If you click on the website (https://drtrozzi.substack.com/p/dr-mccullough-interview), you will hear an interview with Dr. Peter McCullough, that will bring you up to date on what has been happening medically over the past four years and where we are now. As far as I am concerned, Dr. McCullough is one of the best medical doctors in the world on the subject of COVID-19 and the vaccines.

Do you, your family and friends a favor and listen to the hour-long interview. Don't let the past 4 years of propaganda keep you from listening to the interview. Words that have been used against the population and kept them from being rational about the pandemic are:

1. Misinformation
2. Dis-Information
3. Mal-Information
4. Anti-Science
5. Anti-Vaxer
6. Conspiracy-Theory

These same divisive words have been used as far back as the chief propagandist for the Nazi Party, by Paul Joseph Goebbels, to give false information by people in authority, to control the general population.

Chapter 5

How the Media and Government Controlled the Narrative on COVID-19

Since the last chapter dealt with techniques the media, big pharma, and the government used to convince many people to blindly get the COVID-19 vaccine, with most not having informed consent by not being told of all the adverse reactions prior to the injection, we can start here with a list of such reactions presented to the FDA prior to release of the vaccine. The below information was projected on a screen at the FDA by one of the big pharma companies prior to release of the vaccine.

Besides all the adverse physical reactions that might be experienced from the vaccine, the top of the list states DEATH may occur from the vaccine.

In a previous book I wrote titled *Invisible Scars*, I mentioned that many, if not all psychiatric medications have a black box warning issued by the FDA. This warning simply states that the medication may have death as a side effect. It's very interesting that although the COVID-19 vaccine has death as a side effect, the FDA did not issue a black box warning for the COVID-19 vaccine.

Since the COVID-19 vaccine has been released, many of the listed side effects, as well as death, have been seen in those injected. The numbers of adverse reactions are identified in Chapter 4, including those listed by the FDA.

But many individuals deny the adverse reactions were identified.

Denial can be hazardous to your mental and physical health

I once had a Jesuit instructor in undergraduate school who made the comment, "The only mistake I ever made was thinking that I made a mistake."

FDA Safety Surveillance of COVID-19 Vaccines: DRAFT Working list of possible adverse event outcomes
Subject to change

- Guillain-Barré syndrome
- Acute disseminated encephalomyelitis
- Transverse myelitis
- Encephalitis/myelitis/encephalomyelitis/meningoencephalitis/meningitis/encephalopathy
- Convulsions/seizures
- Stroke
- Narcolepsy and cataplexy
- Anaphylaxis
- Acute myocardial infarction
- Myocarditis/pericarditis
- Autoimmune disease
- Deaths
- Pregnancy and birth outcomes
- Other acute demyelinating diseases
- Non-anaphylactic allergic reactions
- Thrombocytopenia
- Disseminated intravascular coagulation
- Venous thromboembolism
- Arthritis and arthralgia/joint pain
- Kawasaki disease
- Multisystem Inflammatory Syndrome in Children
- Vaccine enhanced disease

We all know people like this in our lives and must realize that they choose not to go beyond what they perceive is true for them. They view their truths as universal truth. At times, it is not even worth the time and frustration to talk with them about anything serious. Just stick with the weather and the price of gas. You recognize these people instantly when you mention something, anything, and their first response is, "yeah, I know."

Recently I read an article in *Psychalive* that is very relevant to what is occurring in the world today. Whether you are dealing with political or medical situations, denial may come into play and prevent even the brightest people from seeing things clearly. Denial is a defense mechanism used to dull psychological pain that is caused when our basic and/or higher-level psychological needs are being threatened.

If you view Dr. William Glasser's choice theory psychology as a model, you will see that all human beings have both basic physical needs and higher-level psychological needs. Basic needs are physical: survival from illness and sufficient food, clothing, and shelter. Higher-level needs consist of: 1. Involvement/belonging, 2. Power/self-worth, 3. Fun/learning new information and 4. Freedom to live your life as you desire.

You can determine for yourself if any of your above-mentioned needs are being affected by what is happening in our country today, which may result in your using denial to dull your psychological pain when needs are not being met. But based on what is occurring in the world and in our own country, there will be some people who choose denial to keep an even mental balance in their lives. But the danger is that using denial may go beyond simply not being open-minded and may cause people to distance themselves from friends and relatives who don't share their perceptions and only affiliate with people who do.

To deny another person's perceptions and imply they are wrong, and you are right, will most often lead to more than a simple disagreement. This is what leads to arguments—the denial of allowing a person the freedom (or opportunity) to express what they perceive. "Give me liberty or give me death," in a sense, is what occurs when you try to deprive a person of an inherent human need such as the freedom to think, perceive, and decide. This is why one of the most important things I have taught my patients, interns, etc., is that no two people can view the same thing 100% the same way. As mentioned previously in this book, all humans have unique brains (like their fingerprints) and different life experiences. Every conversation, in fact, becomes a disagreement to various degrees. With this in mind, we must be able to state, "You are right for you, and I am right for me, how can we compromise and negotiate so we can meet somewhere near the center or better?" But when one states, "I am right and you are wrong," the resulting denial of the other's human psychological need becomes an argument that can lead to destructive relationships.

While writing this piece on denial, I happened to attend a car show. At the show, I met two people, one I previously had talked with, and the other was a physician I had never met. The topic got around to the COVID-19 vaccine and when I mentioned its severe side effects, the person I previously knew moaned and immediately walked away. He was in complete denial/ignorance since he had his own unsupported beliefs, and it was too psychologically painful to hear anything different. The physician, on the other hand, was willing to hear information he was not comfortable with and thanked me for the discussion and new information. His training in the past allowed him to be comfortable learning new information, since it made him more effective as a physician. The person who walked away immediately was not confident in his (faulty) knowledge base and information sources, or maybe he was just ignorant, and could not be comfortable learning the truth. The media has created masses of people like this, who have been spoon fed so much misinformation over time, that they perceive it as the truth, and deny reality.

Even Sigmund Freud, many years ago, indicated that "denial is unconsciously choosing to push back on factual truths because to admit them would be too psychologically uncomfortable and require facing the unbearable." Not much different from Glasser's choice theory psychology concepts I described above. When denying, people can refuse to see the other sides of issues, reduce factual information in their own mind, and refuse to reduce other people's responsibility for promoting adverse responsibilities.

Chapter 5

They may acknowledge, at times, the adverse problems revealed, but refuse to blame the parties involved, especially a political party's thoughts or beliefs.

Some believe there is little to worry about so long as some of us are fighting back.

Be mindful not to allow this protective pattern of your ego to morph into potentially disastrous long-term outcomes. You have the choice to wield this defense mechanism in a way that is more helpful than harmful.

Chapter 6

How Does Fear Affect a Person?

I have had several people ask me how fear can affect their physical and mental health. We have all encountered many instances in our lives that demonstrate how fear can be expressed. Scared stiff, scared straight, he/she is scary, if your car doesn't scare you, it doesn't go fast enough, heebie-jeebies, makes my blood run cold, jumped out of my skin, scared out of my wits, scared the living daylights out of me, etc.

Fear can in fact trigger a fight-or-flight response in a person. Although fear is experienced in your mind, it triggers a strong physical reaction in your body. As soon as you recognize fear, the amygdala in your brain goes to work. It alerts your nervous system to go into action. Hormones like cortisol and adrenaline are released and your blood pressure and heart rate increase. Breathing becomes faster and blood flows away from your heart and into your limbs, making it easier for you to start to go into a flight or fight mode. But what happens if your fear response continues in action when there is no immediate cause present? It is well known that when the amygdala senses fear, the cerebral cortex, which is the area of the brain that reasons and provides judgment, becomes impaired and it becomes difficult to make good decisions or think clearly.

As previously mentioned, **reciprocal inhibition** is a psychological term as well as a physiological term, that means you can't have two conflicting emotions or physical reactions occurring at the same time, i.e., happy and depressed. It should be noted that this reaction can be heavily influenced by fear, which causes physiological reactions that interfere with thinking clearly.

This human response is used by people who use fear to control others, since they know people make bad decisions, which they would otherwise not make, when they are afraid. Hence the saying, scarred out of my wits.

An example of this occurred in Nazi Germany prior to, and during, World War II. They instructed their media to state that the Jewish people were diseased. By frightening the German people into fearing that they would contract a disease from this population, it allowed the Nazis to set in motion their plan to exterminate the Jewish population. Because the German people were fearful of catching a disease from the Jewish people, they allowed this catastrophe to occur.

Therefore, as mentioned above, when individuals are highly fearful, they make bad decisions.

This explains how the other factors I previously mentioned most often use fear as the foundation of what they practice, i.e., boiling frog syndrome, brainwashing, gaslighting, etc.

Over these past several years, the media, medical establishment, government, and pharmaceutical companies have been scaring the United States population, indicating that a virus (which without treatment, 99.7% of the general population would be able to overcome) would result in life-threatening consequences.

I have seen many individuals that I considered fearless, locking themselves in their homes and becoming scared, depressed, and anxious about venturing out into the community. They were extremely fearful of the China Flu (COVID-19) that without treatment has a 99.7% survival rate for the general population. These citizens, from all levels of society, allowed themselves to be injected with an experimental gene therapy, cancer treatment drug used in chemotherapy, to prevent contracting the China Flu. (In 2024, the 9th Circuit Federal Court ruled that the COVID-19 Vaccine does not prevent a person from contracting COVID-19 and should not be classified as a vaccine, since the definition of a vaccine prevents a person from getting the disease). Why this is occurring was explained earlier.

The state of fear

When the amygdala senses fear, the cerebral cortex, which is the area of the brain that reasons and provides judgment, becomes impaired, it's difficult to make good decisions or think clearly.

If the general public were not in a state of fear, they would reason that an experimental gene therapy drug, with insufficient testing results, would not be a reasonable choice to fight the flu. Alternatively, a substantial portion of these poor decisions were probably the result of plain old ignorance, which is common in America today.

I have read articles about people experiencing extreme allergic reactions to the current injections, i.e., a nurse being hospitalized and her doctor stating, while she was in bed recovering, that getting the injection was a great choice. Another instance was a nursing mother, who after being injected, lost her baby within days, from a reaction to the vaccine received through the mother's milk. I have had friends state that the injection was great since it got rid of their fear of COVID-19, even though they can still be infected and be contagious.

What always astonishes me is that heart disease is the number one killer in the US, with over 690,000 deaths a year. Worldwide, nearly 18,000,000 people die annually due to cardiovascular diseases, comprising 31% of all global deaths. Why aren't people fearful of dying from heart disease and pursuing safe cures (which do not require injections with severe adverse events) from this disease, such as reducing excessive weight/obesity, exercising, nutrition, etc.? All I can say is to follow the money to answer this question.

For people who are not living in fear, there is information available that will give a broader perspective than the general news source. It is located at VAERS and is co-managed by the CDC & the FDA: The CDC and FDA don't make the information on the vaccine's adverse reactions easy to find, as you can see from the below instructions on how to find how many people died shortly after getting the vaccine shot. If you take the time to read some of the reports, you will see just how they died. It wasn't from car accidents. As they say, where there is smoke there is fire.

Instructions for finding VAERS website

Step 1. Go to https://vaers.hhs.gov. (VAERS is co-managed by the CDC & the FDA).

Step 2. Click on "Search VAERS Data" in the middle of the page.

Step 3. Scroll down to the bottom, and select the final box that says, "I have read and understand the disclaimer."

Step 4. Click "Download VAERS Data."

Step 5. Next to the year 2021, select the link to the Zip file.

Step 6. You will be prompted to complete a Word Verification, then click "Download File".

Step 7. Open your Downloads folder and double click the new VAERS Zip file to unzip the content.

Step 8. The unzipped folder should contain three files—open the first one, 2021vaersdata.csv

. . .

Step 11. In the empty box that will be provided upon making your selection, type the letter "Y" and hit enter.

Step 12. You will see that your chart now has a list of people with the letter "Y", (Yes, have died), under column J.

All these people with a "Y" under the "Died" column suffered death as an adverse reaction to the COVID-19 vaccine; keep in mind that the VAERS site only gets about 10% of the data reported to them.

Also: The European database of suspected drug reaction reports is EudraVigilance, which also tracks reports of injuries and deaths following the experimental COVID-19 "vaccines."

For more information: https://www.primarydoctor.org/covidvaccine

> In the age of information, ignorance is a choice.

Chapter 7

Understanding Negative Projection or Transference as a Possible Reason for Hurtful Behavior

Since we see so much negativity on various media outlets, the below will cover the negative side of the concepts described, although there is a positive side.

With all the angry exchanges we see every day on the news between politicians, news reporters, and people in general, how do we determine the reasons individuals are so angry with each other? If we look closely, we may see the possibility of two psychological constructs occurring called Projection and Transference. By understanding these two psychological concepts, it may help us see what may be occurring and answer some questions we may be asking ourselves, i.e., Why would someone be so angry with the person they are talking to or talking about?

Recently, there was a network news reporter who contracted COVID-19 and had to be quarantined for two weeks in his home. When he returned to work, he was very angry at other people for not being more cautious about COVID-19 exposure, even though he was seen out in public when he was supposed to be restricted to his home. He was guilty himself of doing exactly what he was so angry with others for doing. To mental health specialists, this behavior can possibly be seen as projection on his part. To people in general viewing this behavior, they may simply call it hypocrisy, which is the practice of claiming to have moral standards or beliefs to which one's own behavior does not conform, also known as pretense.

Projection refers to unconsciously taking unwanted emotions, behaviors, or traits you don't like about yourself and attributing them to someone else.

This happens when a reporter, politician, etc., takes a behavior that they have themselves and blames the other person for having the same behavior, when it is not true for the other person.

That's when a neutral observer can see that the projecting person is lying and spreading false information. When you look more closely, the projecting person is truly the person with these behaviors and is placing blame on another person. By doing this, the projecting person feels relieved that the other person is the one with the problem, even though, at a lower or less than conscious level, they know is the trait really belongs to themselves and not the other person.

Transference occurs when a person redirects some of the feelings or desires they have seen in another person in their life to an entirely different person. A person may direct perceptions they have for one person on to an entirely different person. For example, they may have had a father who was mean-spirited and place this perception onto an entirely different person who does not possess this characteristic. Again, a neutral person, observing the individual doing the transferring, may see it as lying and providing false information.

The recent Supreme Court Candidate Confirmation Hearings revealed that possibly some senators redirected some of their negative feelings or desires they have seen in other people in their life onto the candidates. Transference, or possibly simple political hatred, may be occurring in this situation. In any case, when false negative information is attributed to another person, it is hurtful.

I suggest that we look at people in politics, and elsewhere, when we sense they are making false accusations about someone, as possibly demonstrating negative projection or negative transference.

Depression is another behavior that people use to reduce psychological pain caused by many factors I described in previous chapters. It is most often a normal reaction for a person to reduce psychological pain temporarily or long term.

With the COVID-19 Flu outbreak, many people were experiencing depression and inquiring about the best way to deal with it. One of the things that I have told people is that depression is a normal way the body deals with any type of loss. When people experience a loss, whether it be from activities, friends, work, etc., a common way to deal with the psychological pain resulting from the loss is to depress. This can be seen as similar to when someone cuts themselves and scar tissue develops over the cut. Scar tissue is the body's way to temporarily heal and deal with the chance of infection, and is part of the healing process.

Throughout time, depression appears in most everyone's life, whether it be very brief or extended, depending on the actions the person employs. An example of what I am referring to can be seen in the song, "Have Yourself a Merry Little Christmas," written in 1943 during World War II. Depression was a characteristic of the original words in the song, written for Judy Garland to perform in the movie, *Meet Me In St Louis,* in 1944.

As you can see from the original words below, the early 40s, due to the war, was a time that may be seen by some as somewhat like the plague we had been experiencing. This comparison shows that depression is common in people when they lose some of their abilities to meet their higher psychological needs, as they have done in the past. To explain what I mean by a loss, I revert to what I talked about in discussing choice theory psychology and higher psychological needs.

If one looks at the needs that every human being strives to meet in a healthy way every day of their life, you will see that the COVID-19 Flu has most drastically interfered with all four higher-level needs. The need for love/belonging is significantly interfered with, since people aren't able to gather with friends and family as they have in the past. The need for self-worth/power is also interfered with since many people who meet this need through employment and similar activities, are unable to engage in these activities as they did in the past. The need for freedom is immensely interfered with since the government is telling people how to act and what they can and can't do. The need for fun-/pleasure/enjoyment is also not being met as in the past, since there are many restrictions preventing people from meeting this need, such as closing parks and beaches, and closing all the performing arts venues, etc.

The best way to shorten any depression is to look for alternative ways of meeting these needs other than anti-depressant black box warning psychiatric medications that have suicide as one of the first side effects.

Do as Judy Garland did when she refused to sing the original words to the song, because it was too depressing. By doing so, she put the writer of the song in a position where he had to change some of the depressing words. You can see and hear the changes that were made below when Judy Garland sang the revised song in the movie. Also, Frank Sinatra changed the wording further since he wanted to make the song even more consistent with happiness.

Therefore, a lesson from Judy and Frank, make choices in your life that will meet your needs in a more positive way and always remember, happiness is your choice.

Chapter 7

The original words of "Have Yourself A Merry Little Christmas" were:

Have yourself a merry little Christmas,

It may be your last,

Next year we may all be living in the past.

Have yourself a merry little Christmas.

Pop that champagne cork.

Next year we may all be living in New York.

No good times like the olden days,

Happy golden days of yore.

Faithful friends who were dear to us,

Will be near to us no more.

But at least we all will be together.

If the Lord allows.

From now on, we'll have to muddle.

Through somehow.

So have yourself a merry little Christmas now.

So, this Christmas, when you're arguing with relatives about which lyrics are correct, you'll know where the confusion came from.

Judy Garland rendition: https://www.youtube.com/watch?v=MKG5X0QMSWA

Frank Sinatra rendition: https://www.youtube.com/watch?v=pvA7-EjaSPI

Chapter 8

The Loss of Freedom and Its Effects on Human Beings

I have discussed how choice theory psychology's higher human psychological needs are genetically possessed by all human beings (unless there is a genetic defect), with the need to be FREE being one of the essential needs. For me personally, this is my most powerful need that I have been aware of throughout my life.

People are now asking me why they are feeling so depressed and anxious because of what is occurring daily in the United States, such as the China virus, destructive rioting and looting in major cities, increased crime, and even people being extorted to contribute money to Marxist type organizations.

I heard firsthand from an employee of a business owner who received a letter from an organization stating if she put their sign in the window of her store, her customers would feel safe shopping there. This is what the mafia did, and may still be doing, to extort protection money. This is also a common practice of Marxist and Communist organizations. This person was afraid that if she didn't put their poster in the window, this organization would cause problems for her business. But if she did, the next step that this organization could take would be to ask for money, since the poster in the window is a sign that this person was intimidated.

It appears this type of intimidation is happening to larger companies in the United States. It's no wonder that people are feeling that their need for freedom is being lost. They can't do the things the way they did in the past. The psychological reactions of depression, fear, anxiety, and stress are normal reactions to the current abnormal situation.

A way to deal with these unusual circumstances is to discuss alternatives with family and friends and decide upon multiple alternative solutions to deal with these problems. For the businesswoman, she needs to report this extortion to the shopping center security, the local police, and possibly even the FBI, seeking help in dealing with this potential threat.

But what is critical for all people who feel that they are losing their freedom is to educate themselves as to what is going on and why it is happening. Also, to appreciate living in a free country and to do everything in their power to keep their own freedom, as well as the freedom of their country. If people do this with family and friends, then they are meeting their psychological needs in an effective and healthy manner.

Education as to what is occurring is key to maintaining a sense of freedom, and the video from the 1960s, (link at the end) is a very good educational tool one can view to understand what is again being attempted, as it was in the past. Just knowing that it has happened before and that others in our country have dealt with it previously is comforting. The definitions below are also informative and reveal what freedom-depriving countries practice.

Freedom-depriving practices defined

Definitions reveal what freedom depriving countries practice

Merriam-Webster Definitions

Socialism — noun

so·cial·ism | \ ˈsō-shə-ˌli-zəm \

1: any of various economic and political theories advocating collective or governmental ownership and administration of the means of production and distribution of goods.

2a: a system of society or group living in which there is no private property.

b: a system or condition of society in which the means of production are owned and controlled by the state.

3: a stage of society in Marxist theory transitional between capitalism and communism and distinguished by unequal distribution of goods and pay according to work done.

The three main goals of socialism are 1) distribute wealth equally among the people, 2) government control of society and 3) public ownership of most land.

Marxism-Leninism — noun

Marx·ism-Le·nin·ism | \ ˈmɑrk-ˌsi-zəm- ˈle-nə- ˌni-zəm \

A theory and practice of communism developed by Lenin from doctrines of Marx. The political, economic, and social theories of Karl Marx including the belief that the struggle between social classes is a major force in history and that there should eventually be a society in which there are no classes. Lenin (22 April 1870 – 21 January 1924) was a Russian lawyer, revolutionary, and the leader of the Bolshevik party and the October Revolution. He was the first leader of the USSR and the government that took over Russia in 1917. Lenin's ideas became known as Leninism.

Communism — noun

com·mu·nism | \ ˈkäm-yə- .ni-zəm , -yü- \

1a: a system in which goods are owned in common and are available to all as needed.

b: a theory advocating elimination of private property.

2 a: a doctrine based on revolutionary Marxian socialism and Marxism-Leninism that was the official ideology of the U.S.S.R.

b: a totalitarian system of government in which a single authoritarian party controls state-owned means of production

c: a final stage of society in Marxist theory in which the state has withered away and economic goods are distributed equitably.

d: communist systems collectively

An article titled "How Many Did Communist Regimes Murder?" by R.J. Rummel, gives an overview of how brutal Communist regimes have been in the past, with total disregard for human lives. He states, *"Communism has been the greatest social engineering experiment we have ever seen. It failed utterly and in doing so it killed over 100,000,000 men, women, and children, not to mention the near 30,000,000 of its subjects that died in its often-aggressive wars and the rebellions it provoked. But there is a larger lesson to be learned from this horrendous sacrifice to one ideology. That is that no one person can be trusted with unlimited power. The more power the center has to impose the beliefs of an ideological or religious elite or impose the whims of a dictator, the more likely human lives are to be sacrificed."*

What is described above is but one reason, and the most important reason, to support a capitalistic democracy, where people freely vote to choose what their government implements. Even when contingents of a free democracy try to push a Marxist-Communist agenda, it is good to remember what Lincoln said, "You can fool all the people some of the time, and some of the people all the time, but you cannot fool all the people all the time."

Capitalism — noun

cap·i·tal·ism | \ ˈka-pə-tə-.liz-əm , ˈkap-tə- \

An economic system characterized by private or corporate ownership of capital goods, by investments that are determined by private decision, and by prices, production, and the distribution of goods that are determined mainly by competition in a free market.

Choice theory psychology defined

Choice theory psychology—higher human psychological needs common in all human beings.

1. Love and Belonging (family and friends) 2. Self-Worth and Achievement (work, school, etc.), 3. Freedom (do and go where you want) and 4. Fun (learning new information, general pleasures, etc.). The lower basic human needs are food, clothing, and shelter.

If you review the above, you will clearly see why freedom is so important and is the foundation of our country.

"Information is not knowledge. Information alone cannot accomplish goals. Information is not valuable until transformed into knowledge that can be used to achieve an objective." —Albert Einstein, 1950s

Chapter 9

Khrushchev's Advice

To follow up on chapter 8, the information below goes on to explain in more depth the information previously expressed.

Khrushchev's # 1 piece of advice, given in his speech of September 29, 1959, when he generally said the following: "Your children's children will live under communism. By proceeding with small doses of socialism, people become very gullible, and before they know it, socialism turns into full-blown communism…We won't have to fight you, we will conquer you economically… Democracy will cease to work when you take away from those willing to work and give to those who are not."

(Report in Inside Nova, Culpeper Times , https://www.insidenova.com/culpeper/commentary-remember-khrushchev-s-prediction-in-1959/article_ec0cce4e-7d02-11eb-91ea-abdc2533a441.html) "Commentary: Remember Khrushchev's Prediction in 1959" By Francis Updike, March 4, 2021

It should be of note that the current media has attempted to debunk reports that Khrushchev ever made these statements, due to the current political atmosphere's attempt to rewrite history to conform to their political agenda. Knowing the type of person Khrushchev was, from listening to his speech at the UN when he banged his shoe on the table and also almost started WW III by placing nuclear rockets in Cuba, I would go with Frances Updike's commentary. Since so many of the items listed on how to create a communist country are actually happening now in the US, it's better to take the safer course and pay attention to the list of ways to communism, instead of getting into a debate about whether he said them or not. What was said is irrelevant, since the list is something to consider in preventing them from happening either way.

How to create a Socialistic and Communist State

1. **Healthcare** — When you control healthcare you control the people. (i.e., California's Assembly Bill AB 2098)

2. **Poverty** — Poor people will not resist if you are providing everything for them.
3. **Increase debt** — to an unsustainable level, then you can increase taxes and that creates more poverty.
4. **Gun control** — if the citizens cannot defend themselves, then you can create a police state.
5. **Welfare** — control every aspect of people's lives, food, clothing, and shelter and they will become fully dependent on the government.
6. **Education** — control what children learn in school, and then you can control what they think.
7. **Religion** — take away God and have the people only depend on the government for their reasoning and values.
8. **Class warfare** — creates rich and poor classes with no middle class. This way, the government can tax the rich and the poor will support the government for doing so.
9. **Control the media** — and what people are led to believe.

The Lawsuit

If you look at what is occurring now in our society, you get the idea that China and Russia have been attempting to follow the nine rules mentioned above by Khrushchev. Number 1 on his list is **Healthcare** — When you control healthcare you control the people. (i.e., California's Assembly Bill AB 2098).

Attorneys for two doctors had filed a federal lawsuit against the Medical Board of California and State Attorney General Rob Bonta over a freshly signed law that aims to punish physicians for spreading "misinformation" or "disinformation" related to COVID-19.

An injunction stopped this law that the Governor signed, and another law was proposed in its place eliminating it completely. The people had spoken, and action was seen.

"*California legislators have subtly passed a bill that would repeal a law targeting doctors who take a stand against mainstream COVID-19 narratives after previously labeling them as engaging in "medical misinformation." SB 815 declares. "This bill would repeal (AB2098) the provisions that provide that it shall constitute as unprofessional conduct for a physician and surgeon to disseminate misinformation or disinformation related to COVID-19, as provided."*

Chapter 10

The New Art of War

Should I Believe William J. Holstein's Book, *The New Art of War*: China's Deep Strategy Inside the United States?

The last chapter dealt primarily with Russian desires, but this chapter gets significantly more into the Chinese Communist Party and their country being one and the same. We are fortunate to have William Holstein write a book detailing what has been going on in China, since he lived there for many years and spoke the language.

In 2019, I was talking with a friend, who is a retired two-star army general. During the conversation, he told me I should read *The New Art of War* by William J. Holstein (Holstein is an expert on China, living there as a journalist and speaking the language). The General mentioned that he has, in the past, seen combat as an Army Officer and a Green Beret. He stated that as severe as his combat situations were, the only time the hair stood up on his arm was when he read, *The New Art of War*.

After reading the book, I understood the General's concern. Previously, in one of my *Ask the Psychologist* editorials, I wrote:

"Just because you are paranoid doesn't mean they aren't after you."

In this past issue, I discussed many of the topics in the Holstein book.

What got my attention when reading Holstein's book were the following items:

> Holsteins book was written before the recent release of the China Virus, better known as COVID-19. In the book, he quoted the Communist Chinese Party (CCP) as stating their next war **would not** be fought with airplanes and ships, but with biochemical warfare, brainwashing techniques, infiltration of their spies, cyber warfare, etc. One must remember that the Communist Chinese Government

requires all individuals born in China to be, when called upon, agents of the Chinese government. With this in mind, we should look at another exposure in Holstein's book. There are approximately **350,000** students from China in American Universities, and they are mostly taking science-based courses. There are thousands of Chinese Nationals who remain in the United States after they graduate from college and find employment within United States companies. Many of these jobs are highly sensitive defense and/or commercial positions. Most, if not all, have CCP handlers, who could call on them at any time for critical, classified information. If they do not obey, their families in China would experience severe consequences. A few of my friends, who were born in China verified to me that this is true.

China's cyber warfare against the West has long been in effect by including modified computer components capable of spying and degrading our computers. Chinese spying and sabotage have become rampant. It was only discovered within the past several years that the US Navy had these chips in many of their computers monitoring Naval operations. These computers were retrieved, and the bogus chips were replaced. My family member is with a police agency and also informed me they found these Chinese computer chips in their computers and had to buy all new computers. There are still many infected defense contractor computers that retain these cyber warfare chips, but as hard as it was for me to believe, they don't want to spend the money to remove them.

When you think about chemical and biological warfare, you are reminded that the China virus was engineered in Wuhan, China. There is a strong feeling that this virus was purposely released, since the Communist Chinese Party disallowed all air flights out of Wuhan that would land on the Chinese mainland. But flights were allowed to leave Wuhan province and travel all over the world at the same time, thus spreading the virus worldwide. Another fact that concerns me, regarding the Chinese Virus and the related vaccine, was revealed to me by a prominent physician I know, born and educated in China. He has medical colleagues in China that he still communicates with currently. He told me that the Chinese Military does not get the same m-RNA vaccine our military receives. When I asked him why, he stated that it is not safe. He mentioned that Chinese soldiers only get the traditional yearly flu shot.

A large part of China's plan of conquest is propaganda. China has holdings in many news organizations throughout the world and especially the United States. I recently discovered that China provides funding through one of its companies to an American company that does fact-checking for some United States Internet organizations. *(The fact-check company for Facebook Lead*

Stories is run by a long-time CNN employee and is funded partially by a company {Bite-dance} that is owned by the Communist China's Party).

In Holstein's book, he describes how the CCP controls American politicians. A member of the CCP bragged a few years ago at a conference in China about the fact that they could buy most American politicians with enough money. Currently, if you look, it's not necessarily that difficult to find the influence that Chinese money has had on political leaders in our country.

One must remember that the CCP has been at war, actively and passively, with the United States since the late 1940s (Korea, Vietnam etc.). But now, since the release of the Chinese Virus, China has actively been at war with the US, and indeed the world, for the past three years. As the book states, China's CCP sees war as very long term and what they have been doing for years is part of their master plan to take over, not only the US, but the world. Not much different from what past tyrants attempted.

The CCP has been following Khrushchev's advice that I previously mentioned in a speech given in on September 29, 1959, when he generally said the following: (*Worth repeating here*)

"Your children's children will live under communism. By proceeding with small doses of Socialism, people become very gullible and before they know it, socialism turns into full-blown communism."

He stated, "We won't have to fight you, we will conquer you economically.

Democracy will cease to work when you take away from those willing to work and give to those who are not."

How to create a Socialistic and Communist state

1. **Healthcare** — When you control healthcare, you control the people.
2. **Poverty** — Poor people will not fight back if you provide everything for them.
3. **Increase debt** — to an unsustainable level, then you can increase taxes, and that creates more poverty.
4. **Gun control** — if people cannot defend themselves, then you can create a police state.
5. **Welfare** — control every aspect of people's lives, food, clothing, and shelter and they will become fully dependent on the government.
6. **Education** — control what they read and listen to and what children learn in school, and then you can control what they think.
7. **Religion** — Take away God and have the people only depend on the government for their reasoning and values.
8. **Class warfare** — creates rich and poor classes with no middle class. This way, you can tax the rich, and the poor will support the government for doing so.
9. **Control the media** — and what people are led to believe.

If you look at what is occurring now in our society, you get the idea that China and Russia have been attempting to follow the nine rules mentioned above.

Regarding influencing the economy, a recent email I received from a friend gave me a list of United States-based food manufacturers that experienced extreme damage which reduced the amount of food processed. Just today, I went to the grocery store and did not see food items that were there just weeks ago. I could see how this may be related to the CCP's overall plan of creating economic hardships for manufacturers, which is a main emphasis in defeating countries with economic disasters. I can see this happening daily. Yesterday, I had to pay $25.00 for a breakfast meal. I'm sure the restaurant owner would attribute the high price to the increased cost of food. Eventually, people will cut back on eating out if this trend continues. In the past, this restaurant was always full, but now it is mostly empty.

Jim Hoft Published June 11, 2022

A list of America's 98 plants that have been destroyed, damaged, or impacted by "accidental fires," disease, or general causes within the past two years.

With inflation at 40-year highs, this is devastating news. What is going on in America today? For now, you will have to judge for yourself what is happening.

Recently a new book by a China expert was released that supports Holstein's book. It was written by LifeSiteNews: *The Politically Incorrect Guide to Pandemics,* by China expert Steven Mosher, where he blasts the absurd global COVID-19 response and the plot for power that lurks beneath it.

Mosher states, "The World Health Organization's insistence that people stop calling COVID-19 the Wuhan Flu, or the China Virus, is just a clumsy effort to obscure the origins of the pandemic," in what he argues is "part of the WHO's larger effort to cover up China's culpability in general."

Chapter 11

Medicine Cures Diseases of the Body; Wisdom Liberates the Soul of Sufferings

The chapter title is reflective of the work done by Gorgias (485-380 BC), who was a Greek Philosopher, who lived in Leontini Sicily. Below I want to elaborate on what Gorgias knew over 2000 years ago: "*Wisdom liberates the soul of suffering.*"

Effects of brain-altering drugs

Brain-altering legal and illegal medications/drugs are resulting in millions of individuals who are not perceiving clearly, and in instances lead to death.

Part of my work for many years has been to expose the destructive nature of brain-altering psychiatric medications that have black box warnings. I have been making people aware for years of the black box adverse reactions that these drugs have on people. I discussed this briefly in the very well-done documentary, "Hidden Enemy," along with several dozen other professionals. (http://www.cchr.org/documentaries/the-hidden-enemy.html).

I have been a Roman Catholic my entire life, even attending a Jesuit College for undergraduate and graduate studies. In 2016, I received the highest award from the Jesuit College, the University of Scranton, the "Frank O'Hara Award," for living the Jesuit philosophy of "Serving Others". But in all my lectures and 56 years in the mental health field, I have never seen brain-altering psychiatric medications from a religious viewpoint. That all changed over the years, due to my exposure to several people and situations.

On October 18, 2017, I gave a talk in Los Angeles. Preceding me was a Medical Doctor who discussed how rampant the distribution of psychiatric drugs is throughout the world. In Asia, Africa, Europe, etc. These Drugs, as I previously knew were being given to very young children, as well as adolescents and adults, are now more than ever being distributed on a worldwide basis.

The next day, I spoke with my daughter, who works with and teaches young high school age students. She told me that many of these students are being legally given and taking amphetamines (Speed by its street name), because they have been diagnosed with learning disabilities (ADD, ADHD, which I feel are made up labels). I knew this had been occurring, but did not know the extent that many students fake learning problems so they can get these medications legally. These meds are also rampantly distributed among students, from student to student. Also, these medications are known medically to shrink one's brain (confirmed by brain scans). It is known that for many people, these drugs are entry-level drugs, leading to more heavy illegal drugs used later in life.

Over the years, I had the opportunity to speak with a Benedictine Oblate (she works with various people at the Vatican), a psychologist who specializes in brain scans, and a community leader who is heavily involved with the Catholic Church. In all, I spent about eight hours in discussion with these individuals; chief among the subjects was the extensive distribution and the destructive nature of black box (meaning this drug can kill you), brain-altering psychiatric medications.

My feelings prior to these discussions was that the massive **misuse** of these medications was a crime, due to the side effects resulting in many acts of violence and suicide, associated with their usage (As I explained extensively in my #1 Best-Selling Book, *Invisible Scars* www.bartpbillings.com).

But over time, I came to see the massive use of these medications as a crime against humanity. Although people don't necessarily see me as an overly religious person, but mostly as a good person, I will presently attempt to make a religious point on this subject.

With the above in mind, I now see the distribution of these black box brain-altering psychiatric medications as a sin against humanity. If you believe the part of the title which states, "**Wisdom liberates the soul of sufferings,**" then we must look at human beings as having a soul.

If we agree that WISDOM liberates the soul, then we must see that brain-altering drugs (adverse effects include poor judgment and reasoning, etc.), as described above, interferes with people becoming wise, their ability to acquire wisdom, and that these medications, steal one's soul.

If you believe in good (God, based on your religion) and evil (words used to describe evil are Satan, Devil, etc.), then what would be a convenient subversive way for evil to steal one's soul, than to deprive them of their wisdom, with brain-altering drugs. Therefore, I now see **pure evil** attempting to control human beings, by feeding them brain-altering psychiatric medications in massive amounts, to people of all ages throughout the world.

It should also be noted that one of the adverse reactions from the COVID-19 vaccine is death. You now must ask yourself why this vaccine doesn't have a black box warning.

Chapter 12

The Media and Tribalism, is it Good or Bad?

Tribalism is the human tendency to seek out and connect with like-minded people who share common interests, beliefs, or habits. According to Seth Godin, a tribe is a group of people who are connected to one another. With a negative connotation and in a media and political context, tribalism can also mean discriminatory behavior or attitudes towards out-groups, based on in-group loyalty.

I remember one of my college psychology professors telling our class that a sociology course will simply tell us that people live in groups. In a sense, primitive man/woman lived in groups to survive. Every member of this tribe had sets of duties that benefited the total group and helped all survive. Out of this evolutionary process developed the need to have the species survive, and eventually, natural laws for human existence followed.

Natural law is a theory in ethics and philosophy that says that human beings possess intrinsic values that govern their reasoning and behavior. Natural law maintains that these rules of right and wrong are inherent in people and are not created by society, politics, or court judges. The thinking can be deduced that without these natural laws, it would be a matter of time before the human species will become extinct.

It can then be stated that all humans are fundamentally equal and bestowed with an intrinsic basic set of rights that no human can remove. There is a body of unchanging moral principles, regarded as a basis for all human conduct. From the time human beings first walked the earth, they realized that the first example of a natural law includes the idea that it is universally accepted and understood that killing a human being is wrong. However, it is also universally accepted that punishing someone for killing that person is right. Without this recognition, the human groups would eventually disappear, along with their whole species.

Various religions reflect on natural laws for human survival. **The Ten Commandments** reflect the natural moral laws. The natural moral law means the objective moral order created by God. That is, there is a "divine blueprint" or "set of rules" by which people live moral lives. The Ten Commandments teach about respecting God, being honest, honoring our parents, keeping the Sabbath day holy, and being good neighbors, etc. These rules are as important today as they were thousands of years ago.

Those natural rights of life, liberty, and property are protected implicitly in the original US Constitution and are explicitly protected in the Bill of Rights. That right to liberty is the right to do all those things that do not harm another's life, property, or equal liberty. Many scholars, as well as I, think that the idea of natural rights emerged from natural law,

> Therefore, when tribes are harmful, they have negative connotations and are in a one-sided political context. This type of tribalism can mean discriminatory behavior or attitudes towards out-groups, based on in-group loyalty. As a result, they will restrict the natural rights of the out-groups. We have seen this destructive tribalism throughout history, where the result was the violation of the first example of a natural law, the death and punishment of innocent human beings. This especially occurs when various countries with media support helped create Fascism, Socialism, Marxism, and Communism, i.e., Hitler's media, Stalin's media, Mao's, etc.

The major question is, do you see this happening now, over the years in the United States, and if so, are you contributing to a one-side political context?

Currently, we see the major media supporting and helping create extreme leftist organizations.

> Like previous Marxist governments of the past, that eventually failed for the country they were tried in, today's Black Lives Matter, White Supremacist Movements, and ANTIFA groups in the USA and elsewhere, are attempts, thru coercion, intimidation, violence, fabrication, etc., to take control of governments with the help of biased media and sometimes foreign powers. Without distorted reporting, these organizations would cease to exist because true and factual information would demonstrate that they deprive people of their natural laws required for human existence. Pillaging, burning, killing, maiming was often seen in barbaric conquering marauders. Today's laws should prevent these behaviors, but with foreign influences and domestic political motives, at times, the laws are difficult to enforce.

Chapter 12

Referring back to the book I mentioned, *The New Art of War*, you will realize that part of our enemy's war plan is to destroy, from within, by any means, the country they want to conquer.

Chapter 13

First, They Came!

Martin Niemoller (1892-1984), was a prominent Lutheran pastor in Germany, who was a critic of Hitler and came out with the below quote after the war.

"First, they came for the socialists, and I did not speak out—because I was not a socialist.

Then they came for the trade unionists, and I did not speak out—because I was not a trade unionist.

Then they came for the Jews, and I did not speak out—because I was not a Jew.

Then they came for me—and there was no one left to speak for me."

When initially there were physicians advocating for a safe early treatment for COVID-19, not requiring an experimental vaccine, the TRIAD came after them viciously. When you ask what this triad is, you don't have to look far.

Definitions from Oxford Languages

/ ˈtrī.ad /

noun

1. a group or set of three connected people or things.

"the triad of medication, diet, and exercise are necessary in diabetes care"

2. a secret society originating in China, typically involved in organized crime.

The Triad in the US

I sense that the Triad coming after physicians and others exposing the adverse effects of the m-RNA vaccine and advocating the use of successful early treatment were, BIG PHARMA, THE MEDIA, and GOVERNMENT.

I strongly sensed this triad when I initially asked my local medical clinic what the COVID-19 screening test was cycled at by the lab. When they

Chapter 13

couldn't tell me, and the referring physician didn't know, and neither did the local lab, I called the corporate headquarters of the lab in another state. I was told by their science officer that they were instructed to cycle all COVID-19 tests at 45. When I told him at the very beginning of COVID-19, Dr. Fauci said publicly that if the tests were cycled over 35, there would be many false positives. The science officer said cycling at 45 was required by the FDA, and it would be illegal to share this cycling rate with the public. I then asked him if there would be many false positives treated for COVID-19 and even financially reimbursed, assuming they were positive. (i.e. Death from motorcycle was claimed to die from COVID-19). That is when he cut the conversation short One must remember that there were large financial reimbursements for medical facilities expenses if a patient had a primary diagnosis of COVID-19. This reimbursement, I was told, applied to other locations such as funeral facilities.

   I personally experienced this triad when in Oct 2021, my wife and I both tested positive for COVID-19, or as I call it the China flu. Although I was told in the past (1990's) never get another flu shot, due to me contracting Guillain Barre from a tetanus vaccine shot, my family physician forgot he told me this and strongly suggested I get the COVID-19 vaccine. From other physician friends, I was told there was early treatment. One of the physicians I knew was very successful treating COVID-19 patients in Texas and two others were providing early treatment in the San Diego area. All three used the same treatment modalities with success, with next to no hospitalizations or deaths. One of these physicians was Peter McCullough, MD, who was a world-renowned cardiologist, who took time aside to treat COVID-19 patients with his early treatment approach.

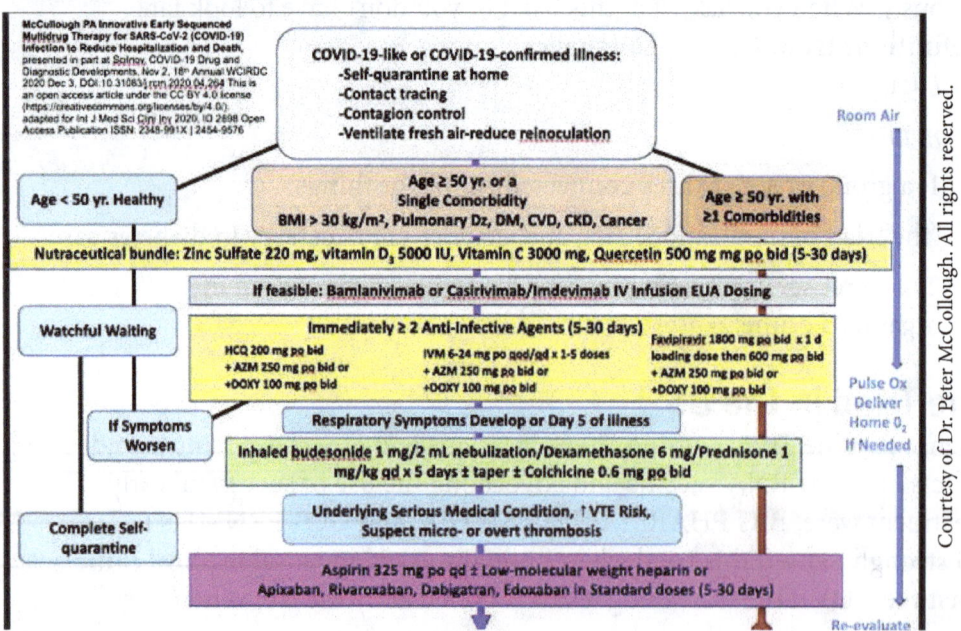

Dr. Peter McCullough's approach

McCullough was one of the best people I could find to answer the above questions about COVID-19 treatment and adverse reactions to the COVID-19 vaccine. He was a physician I personally knew who was a great caring doctor, and who had treated thousands of COVID-19 patients over the past years. I had consulted with him on the phone several times about how he provided early treatment for his COVID-19 patients, with great success. Many of my close family and friends have followed his advice regarding treating COVID-19 without incident. His past practice, as an internist and as a cardiologist for many years, has been highly prized in the past.

When my wife and I were tested positive for COVID-19 in 2021, we used Dr. McCullough's protocol for early treatment and had no more than a head cold for three days and totally recovered. Follow-up blood testing showed natural immunity from this initial flu.

https://www.lifesitenews.com/news/dr-mccullough-shares-protocol-for-covid-and-detoxing-virus-spike-protein/?utm_source=daily-Usa-2023-09-13&utm_medium=email

Some of Dr. Peter McCullough's observations regarding COVID-19 Flu and Vaccine (Permission from Dr. McCullough to include his findings and comments in this book)

— Certain natural enzymes break down the spike protein which is causing long-lasting effects in people who have been infected with COVID-19.

— Dr. Peter McCullough appeared as one of nine panelists in a European Union Parliament session on the WHO.

— He encouraged the EU to completely withdraw from the WHO calling them a harmful bio-pharmaceutical syndicate. He stated, "*The WHO has played an adverse role from the very beginning, deceiving the world on the origins of SARS-CoV-2 . . . they effectively created an environment of scientific nihilism.*

— He described the single biggest problem with the mRNA shot — it's made of a toxic protein that never goes away.

He stated there's not one study showing it leaves the body. He indicated they now have papers by Kestroyuda, who demonstrates the messenger RNA circulating for a month. (That's as long as they've looked!)

— *He also stated the lethal protein from the vaccines found in the human body after vaccination, circulating at least for six months, if not longer, and if people take another injection in another six months,* that's another installation, and more circulating, potentially lethal spike protein.

— McCullough organized officially verified vaccine injuries into four groups, or "domains": cardiovascular, neurologic, blood clots, and immunologic problems.

— He reported that *the spike protein is proven in 3,400 peer-reviewed manuscripts to cause four major domains of disease.*

Number one is cardiovascular disease: heart inflammation, or myocarditis. Every regulatory agency agrees the vaccines cause myocarditis. He is in fact a cardiologist. When there's myocarditis, people cannot exert themselves in athletics, it can cause cardiac arrest. He feels strangely that increased young athletes's cardiac arrests are due to the COVID-19 vaccine until proven otherwise.

Dr McCullough has recently stated separately from the EU talk, that we are witnessing a tsunami of cardiac arrests since the advent of the worldwide mass genetic vaccination program. In virtually every case, the COVID-19 vaccination status is not disclosed to the public. Additionally, the general autopsy can be "normal."

I am commonly asked what a modern COVID-19 vaccine-era cardiac autopsy should look like:
1. Gross inspection, heart aorta, great vessels, lungs, pulmonary arteries.
2. Heart weight <250 g for women, < 350 g for men.
3. Coronary slices for atherosclerosis and thrombus.
4. Myocardial slices for evidence of scar, congenital abnormalities, valvular disease.
5. Myocardial immunohistochemical staining for SARS-CoV-2 Spike Protein and Nucleocapsid, inflammatory cells, amyloid protein.
6. Buccal swab for Arrhythmia and Cardiomyopathy Panel (In Vitae or equivalent).
7. Research assays.

Other diseases that Dr. McCullough mentioned were:
- neurologic disease, i.e. stroke, both acetic and hemorrhagic
- Guillain-Barre syndrome
- ascending paralysis, which can lead to death,
- small fiber neuropathy, numbness, and tingling
- ringing in the ears
- headaches.

He also described the nightmarish, tapeworm-sized types of blood clots that doctors have never squished into before:

- ***Blood clots*** *like we've never seen before. The spike protein is the most thrombogenic protein we've seen in human medicine. It's found in the blood clots. The spike protein causes blood clots. Blood clots bigger and more resistant to blood thinners than we've ever experienced in human medicine. He states he has patients with blood clots going on two years now and they are not dissolving with conventional blood thinners due to these vaccines. We can't get these [clots] out of the body. [Probably because] we can't get the messenger RNA or the spike protein out of the body, as it is continually produced.*

- **Immunologic abnormalities** *Vaccine-induced thrombotic thrombocytopenia and multi-system inflammatory disorder are early-acute syndromes, well-described, published, they have their own acronyms, all agreed-to by the agencies.*

A point McCullough made at the EU: *nobody* is presenting on how successful the shots have been (except possibly at financial conferences). He felt we are **winning** back the mind war.

Having laid out all these potential types of injuries, and knowing most of his audience was probably jabbed, Dr. McCullough then addressed the elephant in the room: Who's next? *So, all of you in the room and all of you listening online are asking, Is it me? Is it a family member? Is it my loved one? Who is going to be the next person to drop after the vaccine? We've seen cardiac arrests now two years after these shots. Two years on, I'm the senior author on the largest autopsy study ever assembled of death after COVID-19 vaccinations. Worldwide, we searched the literature, 600 papers, all the clinical findings, we reviewed them with contemporary knowledge, using experts in pathology and clinical medicine. Our conclusion: 73.9% of the deaths after vaccination are due to the vaccine. When it's suspected myocarditis, it's 100% of the time that it's due to the vaccine.*

Dr. McCullough's warning to the ministers:
- Don't believe the latest fake narrative that "long covid" is causing the excess deaths: The first false narrative was the virus is unassailable, we have to stay in lockdown and be fearful.
- The second false narrative is taking a vaccine, it's safe and effective.
- The third false narrative is: it's not the vaccine causing these problems, it's covid. Don't fall for the false narrative. The medical literature now is compelling. The Bradford-Hill criteria for causality has been fulfilled. The vaccines are causing this enormous wave of illness.
- He said the studies are showing that somewhere between 4% and 7% of the jab batches account for almost all officially recognized jab injuries. So, regarding the recognized domains of injury, there's a good chance that any

person got a safe batch with no reported injuries at all (about a third) or even more likely, a batch with only very rare injuries.

Now one can see why the TRIAD went after Dr. McCullough so vehemently. He and a significant group of physicians adhere to his beliefs. He appears to be the leading physician to shed light on COVID-19 and the Vaccine that accompanies its spread. Is there any wonder that his past reputation has been wrongfully damaged, employment threatened, and his latest book interfered with, as described below?

The excerpt below was sent out by Dr. McCullough regarding his current book. Again, we see the Triad in action.

Is this David vs. Goliath or just a fluke? After the sudden removal and subsequent reinstatement of *The Courage to Face COVID-19*, the Amazon content review process has us concerned about Big Tech's boot on the neck of free speech. Eighteen months after releasing the book, having earned a 4.9/5 Amazon rating and over 1,000 5-star reviews, Amazon's sudden ban is a mystery. Despite our multiple entreaties for clarification, Amazon's content review department was unable or unwilling to specify what it had suddenly found "offensive" about the book. After appealing the decision multiple times and hearing nothing but crickets we announced the ban and our community launched into action. We heard many reports of our supporters writing to Amazon, opening customer support tickets, and airing public concern through social media. After this public rebuke, we finally received a response from Amazon, "We reviewed a recent decision to remove *The Courage to Face COVID-19* and found that it was removed in error. We apologize for the inconvenience this caused.

Is Big Tech doing its best to censor the truth? Are they finally caving to the pressure of our organized voice? Was it truly a fluke? We may never know, but we are grateful Amazon made the decision to reinstate the book and for all the people who assisted in that effort.

In closing this chapter, I must express my reaction regarding Dr. McCullough. The past two years, I have talked with Dr. McCullough more than once and was always impressed with his knowledge and his successful treatment of hundreds of his COVID-19 patients, as well as his success with his early treatment program. I have been in the health field for over 55 years and have met thousands of physicians. I can say there are very few who can compare with Dr. McCullough's caring, knowledge, experience, and tenacity.

As the old saying goes about medical back bitters (Back Biter—to say mean or spiteful things about a person who is not present), they "could not shine his shoes," as I have stated to a few of his critics in the past.

Remember what Khrushchev said. How to create a Socialistic and Communist state: Number 1 on his list, Healthcare—When you control healthcare you control the people.

Chapter 14

You Can't Fool All of The People All of The Time

—attributed to Abraham Lincoln

This is the reason we will always have people strive for a positive and honest country and media.

Why is it impossible to "Fool All of The People All of The Time"? The same reason why a dictatorial government eventually fails over time. Based on choice theory psychology, all human beings have the same basic physical and higher psychological needs built into their genetics that have evolved over millenniums. If these intrinsic needs did not evolve, the human species would not have continued to exist.

Humans needed to band together for survival from wild animals, thus over time, **love/belonging** became part of a human's makeup.

While providing food, clothing, shelter, tools, etc. to survive, the need for **achievement/power** became ingrained.

Being free to live in safe locations that provided continued opportunities for food, clothing and shelter evolved into a need for **Freedom**.

And last, the need to learn new information while enjoying each other became a need for **Fun.**

Today, every human being, in one way or another, wakes up every day seeking ways to meet these basic and, in most cases (if they don't spend all their time seeking food, clothing, and shelter), they then move on to meeting their higher psychological needs. Meeting these needs can be interfered with when a person has a genetic defect, or the natural laws of human existence get violated.

Natural laws indicate that human beings possess intrinsic values that govern their reasoning and behavior. They state that rules of right and wrong are inherent in people and are not created by society or court judges. The Ten Commandments are based on natural laws for human existence as well as most of the US Constitution.

Whatever a government does to influence its population negatively, the people will sense, eventually, that it is not need-satisfied. The most powerful feeling of loss of a higher need is the loss of freedom. People can give away their freedom to a government for only so long, but will sense there is something missing and wrong. Eventually, they won't give it away indefinitely, even if it takes generations, because over time, it becomes too psychologically painful for them and their descendants to continue living. As the saying goes, "Give me liberty or give me death." —Patrick Henry

I recall a patient who was a minister by profession who came to see me for marital counseling. He had been married for 50 years and stated, throughout his total marriage, he always gave his wife everything she wanted, even if he didn't agree. He said he was tired of doing this and wanted his freedom back to be his own person. I explained that his wife never took his freedom away from him, but for 50 years he gave her his freedom. When he realized this, it was a simple matter of taking it back, he then moved forward in his relationship.

Another example of *apparently* giving freedom away was explained to me by a POW friend of mine. Although he was locked in a small cell and tortured often, he never stopped thinking about what he wanted. He was not free physically, but in his mind, he was free to think whatever he wanted to at any time. He would tell his captors what they wanted to hear, but not what he was really thinking. It always interests me that no prisoner in Vietnam, while in captivity, ever committed suicide (revealed to me by this prisoner group's representative after they returned home). This was not the case when they got home, since some of them were given brain-altering, black box warning psychiatric medications for post-traumatic stress. These drugs were given to some because they were seen as having a disorder (PTSD) and not having primarily a normal reaction to an abnormal situation (PTS) in their life. Here again, we see adverse reactions to these drugs, being suicide ideation, depression, homicide, etc. A previous book I wrote, titled *Invisible Scars*, deals with how to treat individuals in this situation, without giving them brain-altering drugs. The treatment is basically integrative therapy.

It becomes very difficult to look toward people we trust who have a positive influence in our life and country. It is factitious to say Mother Theresa is no longer with us to trust and value, and it is not readily obvious if there are people in our society that compare. Just the opposite is true when we get bombarded with names of individuals at the other end of the spectrum. Just today, while writing this chapter, I received an email from a person forwarding me a list of the ten worst people over the past years in the US.

John Hawkins, a retired US Army intelligence officer, emailed an acquaintance his list of the worst 10 people in past years in our country. Lists like this are much easier to come by than lists of the top 10 most beneficial people. His list is composed with number one being the worst. This list will demonstrate how easy it is to criticize people, but where is the best people list over the past decades?

Below this list of negative examples, I will discuss how to come up with people you trust as being positive and the best.

10) Mark Felt

9) Bill Ayers

8) Teddy Kennedy

7) Walter Cronkite

6) Bill and Hillary Clinton

5) Valerie Jarrett

4) Jimmy Carter

3) Lyndon Johnson

2) Barack Hussein Obama

1) Worst American is John Kerry

Dishonorable Mentions! (Just missed the list)

John Brennan

Jane Fonda Robert

Arthur Ochs Sulzberger, Jr.

Frank Marshall Davis

Special recognition goes to George Soros

DA Chesa Boudine

Involvement lists

Now let's get to what I perceive is the best way to identify the people in your life you can trust, with their caring and opinions. There is not a list like the bad people list above, but a list that is different for every person looking to make one. That is because most people don't have to look beyond their own family and friends. In some cases, some of these people are paid therapists.

of the information I provide in this book and in my previous book, *Invisible Scars*. It was an honor for me to receive the Human Rights Award from the International Citizens Commission on Human Rights in 2014 for my past work reflected in the documentary and my book, *Invisible Scars*.

In the documentary, I stated:

"We have never drugged our troops to this extent and current increases in suicide is not a coincidence."

"Why hasn't psychiatry in the military been relieved of command of mental health services?"

"In any other command position in the military, there would have been a change of leadership."

"Why hasn't psychiatry in the military been relieved of command of Mental Health Services?"

Did it ever cross anyone's mind why Veteran Suicides have not decreased in over 20 years? I was just thinking about this after reviewing suicide incidents, etc., information.

The information below reflects what I think (I'm not a statistician) the government generally saves, each time a veteran commits suicide, in regard to pensions and disability (not counting medical care, Soc. Sec, etc.).

I don't want to — and hate — to look at the below information as to a possible reason more is not being done to reduce the suicides of our veterans (over 8,000 this past year).

Also, why the government is not admitting that psychiatry (mostly utilizing black box warning, brain-altering psychiatric medication, with the main side effects being suicide), the profession that is in charge of mental health, is being allowed to continue to fail in saving lives and has not been fired and replaced by the more suitable profession of Physical Medicine & Rehabilitation (Physiatry, Medical Doctor in PM&R).

In 2013, the United States Department of Veterans Affairs (VA) released a study that covered suicides from 1999 to 2010, which showed that roughly 22 veterans were dying by suicide per day, or one every 65 minutes. Some sources suggest that this rate may be under-counting suicides.

According to the most recent report published by the VA in 2016, which analyzed 55 million veterans' records from 1979 to 2014, the current analysis indicates that an average of 20 veterans a day die by suicide.

The Government Accountability Office study found that of $6.2 million set aside for suicide prevention media outreach in fiscal 2018, only $57,000 — less than 1% was actually spent.

Even if you look at an average of 20 suicides a day for the past 20 years, this totals 146,000 for 20 years (likely more).

2019 VA Veteran Medical benefits (https://militarybenefits.info/va-disability-rates/)

2019 DOD retirement pension (https://www.military.com/benefits/veteran-benefits/veterans-pensions.html)

Consider this:

— A single Veteran's (not counting dependents) pension averages $13,536 a year (low end).

— An average of a veteran receiving 30% disability comes to $5,136 per year (100% disability averages $36,684 per year).

Based on the above numbers, each veteran that commits suicide saves the government, on the low average side, $18,672 per year in pensions and disability (not counting medical treatment costs, Social Security, etc.)

Over 20 years, the government saves about $373,440 (retirement and disability combined only) **per each veteran who commits suicide**.

For 20 years, if you add 146,000 total veteran suicides in 20 years (low estimate) and government benefits not paid of $18,672 for each veteran that committed suicide.

The total savings for the government for 20 years, for all Veteran suicides, is in the millions of dollars and more.

It's just something that all citizens should think about!

Recent interesting TV media on the subject

This below TV series shows episodes for 2019, #19, #20 & #21 Seal Team, exposed psychiatry, basically contributing to a vet's suicide, by prescribing multiple brain-altering psychiatric meds at a VA. This was done on a national major network TV show (CBS), that coincidentally, so happens to be extremely true to life and parallels actual real suicides happening every day, which was depicted precisely in these episodes. I have personally seen this exact occurrence happen, even the same dialogue, more than once, in my work with vets.

Seal Team Episode April 24, 2019, & May 1 & 8, 2019" Medicate and Isolate" Season 2 Episode 19, 20 & 21 (https://www.cbs.com/shows/seal-team/video/qZjmtSyA6xv8_IV_fZwgZvb35N_7McBM/seal-team-medicate-and-isolate/);

The writer of the *Seal Team* episodes had great insight on the issue and more than likely, got his information from a veteran who has been there.

Also, a *Fox News* interview Apr 24, 2019, with ***Shannon Bream, with the then-current Secretary of the VA, Robert Wilkie (https://www.youtube.com/watch?v=sGoBBUKdZeE) at 30.40 minutes into the show.

Shannon Bream did a great job with Sec. Wilkie, expressing her thoughts about veteran suicides and treatment and asked why the VA is not doing more.

She also quoted Congressman Greg Stube of Florida, who is stating that the VA needs to improve what it is doing for Veterans.

Also on *Fox News* on May 23, 2019, Harris Faulkner interviewed Sec Robert Wilkie (https://www.foxnews.com/politics/va-sec-wilkie-weve-changed-out-leadership-at-va-centers-proposed-largest-budget) and he said that there is no commonality for the veteran's suicides.

Obviously, due to the influence of Big Pharma, he avoided the commonly used brain-altering black box warning psychiatric medications, that have suicide as one of the adverse reactions.

Also not mentioned was the fact that the veteran's choice program (a vet's ability to seek treatment outside the VA) is up to VA staff to make the choice, ultimately, since they must approve private medical treatment payment. I have seen this firsthand, with a vet I am advocating for at present.

***As of 5-20-19, The TV interview with Shannon Bream was taken off *YouTube*. HMMMMMMM. Wonder why?

NOTE* 383,947 TBI's since the year 2000 — Anyone with a TBI has the potential for suicide, four times more than a person with no TBI. Now combine this potential, with that person being prescribed a brain-altering psychiatric medication, with suicide being one of the first major side effects and now you can exponentially multiply the number by four, with no one knowing how much. This is a major factor when considering suicide rates for anyone with a TBI.

Although, there were times that some media reporters discussed suicide and possible contributing factors from brain-altering medications, my observations were that it was a one-time brief discussion only. There was never any significant follow-up reporting. Could this be because well over 50% of a TV network's revenue comes from Big Pharma. To my way of thinking, if an on-air TV host gets into this area, the producers remind them to pull back. That was the reason I was shocked when the TV series, *Seal Team*, was so transparent depicting a Navy Seal's suicide over a 3-episode period and one of the actor's lines was that the government let him down.

Chapter 15

A few years back, I was approached by a group that worked with vets, asking me how we could garner the general publics and the government's attention regarding the large number of veteran suicides. I suggested that they obtain 22 Military Funeral Caissons, drawn by horses, and march them by the White House, stating this is the number of veteran suicides on that day alone, with a parade of people carrying signs behind them with the names of each vet that committed suicide (8,030) that year.

If this could ever be possible, the citizens, media, and the government would get the message.

Chapter 16

The Media, Big Pharma, and Politicians

Do the media, big pharma, and politicians truly report on actual causes of mass shootings?

Is there a solution for preventing purchases of firearms by individuals with mental disorders?

Most people don't know that a large majority of mass shooters/killers were taking brain-altering, **black box warning psychiatric medication or illegal brain-altering drugs, either before the shootings or during the shootings**. Later in this chapter, I will get more into the details of this factor.

I want to start right off with stating psychiatric medical prescription (black box warning brain-altering Psychiatric Medication) and illegal brain-altering drugs are why there are so many school shootings in the past 50 years.

A reasonable solution

I offer a solution for preventing purchases of firearms by individuals on brain-altering drugs with mental disorders, who may present a danger if allowed to possess a firearm.

A reasonable and inexpensive approach would be as follows:

All pharmacists, filling a prescription for a black box, brain-altering psychiatric medication, who normally enter the patient's name into their computer, would at the same time be linked to the Alcohol, Tobacco, Firearms Dept. (ATF), Department of Justice (DOJ) or FBI's database. Once in the ATF, DOJ, and FBI system, the person's name would be sent to every firearms retailer in the United States, putting the name on a "cannot buy a firearm" list.

This way, if the person named on the DOJ "cannot buy" list comes into a gun store to purchase a weapon, the salesperson would simply say their name is on a "cannot buy" list. The list gives no reason, due to confidentiality, and if the person on the list wants to know why they can't purchase a firearm, the salesperson would simply give them the contact information at DOJ to get an explanation.

I would also recommend that if a relative, with the same last name of the person on the list, comes in to purchase a firearm, they should be informed that their relative should not have access to the firearm and that they themselves would be liable if this occurs.

Some may say that this may breach confidentiality, but in California and other states, systems are already in place, where if a person has the potential to harm themselves or others, it gets reported beforehand to the proper agency.

A good example is when a person is considered to have a lapse of consciousness due to some type of brain impairment. The physician has a responsibility to report this person to the appropriate source, so the information gets to the Department of Motor Vehicles.

For example: "California Health and Safety Code, Section 103900 states:

(a) Every physician and surgeon shall report immediately to the local health officer in writing, the name, date of birth, and address of every patient at least 14 years of age or older whom the physician and surgeon has diagnosed as having a case of a disorder characterized by lapses of consciousness. However, if a physician and surgeon reasonably and in good faith believes that the reporting of a patient will serve the public interest, he or she may report a patient's condition even if it may not be required under the department's definition of disorders characterized by lapses of consciousness pursuant to subdivision (d).

(b) The local health officer shall report in writing to the Department of Motor Vehicles the name, age, and address, of every person reported to it as a case of a disorder characterized by lapses of consciousness.

(c) These reports shall be for the information of the Department of Motor Vehicles in enforcing the Vehicle Code and shall be kept confidential and used solely for the purpose of determining the eligibility of any person to operate a motor vehicle on the highways of this state.

(d) The department, in cooperation with the Department of Motor Vehicles, shall define disorders characterized by lapses of consciousness based upon existing clinical standards for that definition for purposes of this section and shall include Alzheimer's disease and those related disorders that are severe enough to be likely to impair a person's ability to operate a motor vehicle in the definition.

Another system that is already in place, that is even more closely related to potential dangers of prescription brain-altering psychiatric medications in California is called the Controlled Substance Utilization Review and Evaluation System (CURES) Program.

This program is as follows:
State of California Department of Justice, Office of the Attorney General

The Department of Justice (DOJ) and the Department of Consumer Affairs (DCA) are pleased to announce that the state's new Controlled Substance Utilization Review and Evaluation System – commonly referred to as **"CURES 2.0"—went live on July 1, 2015.** This upgraded prescription drug monitoring program features a variety of performance improvements and added functionality.

The Controlled Substance Utilization Review and Evaluation System (CURES) is a database containing information on Schedule II through IV controlled substances dispensed in California. It is a valuable investigative, preventive, and educational tool for the healthcare community, regulatory boards, and law enforcement.

Therefore, as one can see, mechanisms are already in existence that can be slightly altered to add brain-altering psychiatric medications. There are actually some brain-altering psychiatric medications (Controlled Substance) on the CURES list that are already identified as Schedule II controlled substances; to mention a few, i.e., Amphetamine – Adderall, Dextroamphetamine (Dexedrine), Lisdexamfetamine (Vyvanse) used for the treatment of ADHD and narcolepsy. Also listed is Methylphenidate (Ritalin, Concerta), Dexmethylphenidate(Focalin), for treatment of ADHD, narcolepsy. Additionally, this applies to Methamphetamine for treatment of ADHD, severe obesity. There are many more brain-altering medications prescribed by physicians, being used for mental health patients, on this schedule II list.

As you can see from the above, there are already systems in place that can be added to, that can identify individuals that have a mental disorder, that are on brain-altering psychiatric medications. By implementing my suggested above program as prescribed, the number of people with mental disorders having access to legally purchasing a firearm would be dramatically reduced.

Also, I feel that the FDA should have the pharmaceutical companies, include in their **Medication Guide**, *which patients and their families are supposed* *to be given*, by the physician prescribing brain-altering *black box* psychiatric medications, the following information: **Individuals taking this medication should not have access to firearms.**

This information is a portion of copyrighted material from the *Invisible Scars* book by Bart Billings, PhD.

Also in the book, this subject was covered by the award-winning journalist David Kupelian as documented in his website article, "A Giant, Gaping Hole in Sandy Hook Reporting". He stated, "It is indisputable that most perpetrators of school shootings and similar mass murders in our modern era were either on, or just recently coming off, psychiatric medications."

Mr. Kupelian gave me permission to reprint his findings in *Invisible Scars*," which included a long list of names of mass shooters, brain-altering medications/drugs they were using, and the location of the shootings.

The Columbine killer

Columbine mass-killer, Eric Harris, was taking Luvox. Like Prozac, Paxil, Zoloft, Effexor, and many others, a modern and widely prescribed type of antidepressant drug called selective serotonin reuptake inhibitors, or SSRIs. Harris and fellow student, Dylan Klebold, went on a hellish school-shooting rampage in 1999, during which they killed 12 students and a teacher, and wounded 24 others, before turning their guns on themselves. Luvox manufacturer, Solvay Pharmaceuticals, concedes that during short-term controlled clinical trials, 4 percent of children and youth taking Luvox–that's 1 in 25–developed mania, a dangerous and violence-prone mental derangement characterized by extreme excitement and delusion. There are many other examples similar to this one in *Invisible Scars*.

With most Americans reeling from the recent spate of mass shootings that tragically took so many lives, many diverse "solutions" are being proposed by legislators, media, and the mental health industry. Yet none addresses causality: namely, what could cause an individual to lose all sense of humanity to carry out such unimaginable acts?

While it is true that many factors can contribute to mass murder, violent crime, and suicide, one well-documented fact is omitted from the press, and of course, the mental health industry "experts," the latter is demanding millions more dollars to "prevent" mass shootings when it's known their psychiatric drugs can cause it! A percentage of the population taking these drugs become manic, psychotic, violent, and homicidal. All of these adverse reactions should be identified when the medication is prescribed.

With 80 million Americans taking these drugs, clearly not everyone will experience violent reactions. But what drug regulatory agency warnings confirm is that a percentage of the population *will*. And no one knows who will be next. This is the game of Russian roulette that is part and parcel of the psychiatric drug industry and its relationship with Big Pharma.

I recall the onset of this symbiotic relationship.

When I was an Army Officer in the Medical Service Corps, I was called to a meeting with other Army psychologists and psychiatrists. At the meeting, the Chief Army Psychiatrist issued a warning. He stated that the major medical insurance companies will no longer pay for long-term psychotherapy i.e. psychoanalysis, which could last as long as once a week for years. Instead, they will only pay for short-term therapy, most often performed by psychologists, social workers, and various counselors.

He told the psychiatrists that unless they can distinguish themselves from the other mental health groups, they will lose their profession. He stated that since they had MD degrees, they were the only mental health group that could prescribe medication. Well, as we see years later, Big-Pharma came to psychiatry's rescue. The more psychiatric labels that psychiatry came up with, the more medications that Big Pharma could develop, regardless of if they were effective and regardless of adverse reactions.

So, as you can see from all the above, our government officials need to focus on brain-altering Psychiatric Medication Control instead of Gun Control. As I explained to a friend, "I have a gun that sits quietly in a corner of my closet, and it never went out for a walk and injured anyone." But if I started taking one or more psychiatric medications (Even more unpredictable in combinations since there is no telling what the side effects will be), any instrument, i.e. a car, knife, gun, hammer, etc. can turn into the weapon that injures others or myself.

Chapter 17

The Homeless Problem

Is the media reporting the government's lack of a solution for the homeless problem? What worked in the past for dealing with the homeless problem can be effective now.

When I moved to California in 1969, I worked extensively with the homeless at Mendocino State Hospital and had an office in Santa Rosa, California. Most of the people I saw were from San Francisco (which is about 60 miles south) and were picked up by the police and transported to Mendocino State Hospital (About 60 miles north of Santa Rosa). Most patients from San Francisco who were taken to the hospital had a diagnosis of alcoholism or illegal substance abuse, with many being homeless. At that time, these people were called *vagrants*—a person without a settled home or regular work who wanders from place to place and lives by begging, stealing, etc. This population now, to be politically correct, are referred to as *homeless*.

In San Francisco during this period, it was illegal to be a vagrant on the streets, since most of these homeless had physical, mental, emotional, and/or substance abuse problems. The police issued a 5250 or 14-day hold to get the person the help they needed. The determination at that time was that the person was a danger to self or others. Additional holds occurred, once the first 14-day hold expired, if the patient continued to meet criteria for involuntary hospitalization, thus the treatment team may extend the hold. Another 14-day hold may be placed at which time a new PC Hearing would take place.

Many lives were saved by the above-mentioned procedure that I personally observed. What occurred when the person was taken to Mendocino State Hospital was as follows:

1. A diagnosis was made so the person could be placed in an appropriate treatment program.
2. All physical problems were immediately treated.

3. Appropriate food, clothing, and living accommodations were provided (basic psychological needs met).
4. Appropriate therapy programs (to meet the four higher level psychological needs) were instituted, with a large variety of treatment modalities from Alcoholics Anonymous-type programs, behavior modification, transactional analysis, reality therapy, Native American, etc. Only limited use of any brain-altering psychiatric drugs was advised, since they would cloud a patient's judgement. Peer groups worked effectively if led by a skilled trained therapist (ex-patients were hired, but were not effective, since they would be more or less, a paid patient. For an ex-patient to be hired, it was recommended that they leave the hospital and get a regular non-mental health job and take college classes in this field).
5. Each of the above programs had their own separate building and patients took pride in what program they were living in. This was readily observable when each program would send representatives to the weekly group therapy meeting, to determine who was ready to be referred to the California Dept. of Rehabilitation, DOR, (office and counselors located within hospital, in their own hospital building) for acceptance into their program for training, job placement, on-the-job training, or education, including college. All these services, plus more, were totally free, and patients worked hard to be accepted.
6. When a patient became a client of DOR, they would make plans to leave the hospital and live in a halfway house with other patients. There would be group therapy sessions in the evenings run by county social workers. The living facility was paid for by the patients, since they received a social security disability check each month.

I personally did a research project that showed that therapy and vocational training being done simultaneously was more effective than either alone. This validated itself, when most patients eventually left the halfway house with a job or moved into a college program, where they became independent, living on their own in a private apartment or home.

The inhumane closure of mental hospitals

This program ended when politicians decided that people in mental hospitals had the legal rights to live in the community, even if they were not physically or mentally ready to do so.

By closing state-run mental hospitals, the states projected they would save much money, which turned out to be a fallacy and inhumane.

The solution, now, would be to establish facilities, like the state hospitals of the past, and provide funding for the homeless population, which has been described above. There are many vacant, abandoned military facilities that could be remodeled and staffed with people who can provide the above services. Let's not forget that each state has a Vocational Rehabilitation Agency, mostly funded by the government, to work with the disabled community, as it did in the 60s and 70s and back to the 1920s.

Also, let's not forget that there were many people from WWI living on the streets after the war, when the Smith Fess Act was passed by congress in 1920. Today, it is called the National Vocational Rehabilitation Act (NVRA), with funds for every state to work with the disabled populations, which most of today's homeless qualify for.

Laws need to be changed now (vagrancy laws), to help get the homeless into treatment and vocational programs, and State and Federal agencies need to do their jobs, as they were directed to do in the 1920s, since the NVRA gets re-certified on a regular basis and exists today.

In the early 1990s, I actually wrote the position paper for a congressman (chairman of the committee) to re-certify the NVRA at that time. Then, one of my major goals was to establish higher national educational levels of staff working for the agencies. Currently, we have more highly educated counselors working in all state agencies. But the problem is that the people running federal and state governments aren't utilizing this agency as it was used with success in the past. As a famous management expert, Dr. W. Edwards Deming, (named an ASQ Honorary member in 1970 for his role as adviser, consultant, author, and teacher to some of the most influential businessmen, corporations, and scientific pioneers of quality control, is the most widely known proponent of statistical quality control) once said, "Ninety-four percent of any organization's problem is management."

If the media in the US was doing its job now, which in a democracy, is to honestly, without bias, report on government shortfalls, we would all know what humanely needs to be done for the homeless on our streets.

Chapter 18

How Does the Media Contribute to Human Suffering?

Why do people join hurtful gangs that inflict human suffering? This question is even more relevant now that we are watching riots on TV in many parts of our country. Violent behavior is being demonstrated by what can be called gangs. One that is frequently involved is ANTIFA, which can be described for the most part as a group of individuals that tend to hold anti-authoritarian and anti-capitalist views, with their views leaning toward Communism, Marxism, Anarchism, Socialism, etc.

This group is militant in nature and does get involved in physical altercations and property destruction. Their symbols and leanings go back to a German movement called ANTIFA. This movement is contrary to the democracy the US stands for, but often, the US media glorifies this behavior to the point of announcing when groups will gather prior to a so-called demonstration.

One needs to distinguish between a demonstration, rioting, and looting, regardless of what the media calls it. By the media not clearly distinguishing between these activities, they may glorify potential destructive behavior, resulting in violence and destruction. If the media didn't, more or less, advertise for everyone to see on TV, resulting in glorifying these activities, then needless damage and injuries could be avoided. This goes back to the saying about what one might do for their "fifteen minutes of fame." The media provides this opportunity if it results in increased viewership, which the media sells to sponsors.

At times, people reporting for the media get inappropriately caught up in the frenzy of what they are reporting, lose sight of fair and honest reporting, and get into the realm of entertainment. Their behavior is not always appropriate. I recall years ago, watching the Olympics when a terrorist group attacked members of the Israeli wrestling team. Prior to the attack, the Olympic announcer exhibited an appropriate amount of excitement for the games, but when he was reporting the unexpected violence, he was twice as animated . This was a very sad situation that was tragic, and his behavior should have reflected the moment. This was the first thought in my life about the media glorifying criminal behavior by how they were reporting it.

Let's be clear:

Demonstrations (or protesting) are a form of activism, usually taking the form of a public gathering of people in a peaceful rally or walking in a march. Thus, their opinion is demonstrated to be significant by gathering in a crowd associated with that opinion. Demonstrations are peaceful in nature and don't have a purpose to injure or damage people or property. Martin Luther King, Jr. set the example for peaceful demonstrations and practiced his first amendment right.

A riot is a form of civil disorder commonly characterized by a group, lashing out in a violent public disturbance, with no focused purpose, except they are against authority, property, or people. This is criminal behavior and not a first amendment right.

One explanation of why people riot can be explained by *De-Individualization theory*, (enhanced recently by wearing medical masks) which states that in typical crowd situations, factors such as anonymity, group unity, and arousal can weaken personal controls (e.g., guilt, shame, self-evaluating behavior) by distancing people from their personal identities and reducing their concern for social evaluation. This lack of restraint decreases individual sensitivity to the environment and lessens rational forethought, which can lead to antisocial behavior. More recent theories have stated that De-Individualization Theory hinges upon a person being unable, due to the situation, to have strong awareness of their self as an object of attention. This lack of attention frees the individual from the necessity of normal social behavior.

Riots typically involve theft, vandalism, and destruction of property, public or private (arson causes the most damage). The property targeted varies depending on the riot and the inclinations of those involved. Targets can include shops, cars, restaurants, state-owned institutions, police, and religious buildings. When interviewed during a riot, participants may not give a specific reason for their behavior, except generally stating that it is an opportunity to get property for free (theft). The people generally victimized during a riot come from all levels of society—their race, religion, and nationality don't matter to the rioters.

Looting, also referred to as sacking, ransacking, plundering, despoiling, despoliation, and pillaging, is the indiscriminate taking of goods by force where law and civil enforcement are temporarily ineffective or when rioting occurs. The proceeds of all these activities can be described as booty, loot, plunder, spoils, or pillage.

I'm sure there are many gangs out there that look for opportunities to take advantage of peaceful demonstrators.

Who becomes a gang member?

If a person cannot meet their basic and higher needs as previously discussed in this book, each day, in a healthy manner, then that person looks for alternative ways of meeting their needs, which may not be constructive.

The point is that these basic and higher psychological needs will and must be met, regardless of what choices are made (choice theory psychology).

In the past, while growing up, people usually learned how to meet their psychological needs from the people who surrounded them, whether it be families, relatives, friends, teachers, etc. Presently the media is another source that a person is exposed to that influences need-fulfilling choices. The problem with information from the media is that it is inconsistent and not reliably truthful. In my past psychology classes, I was told that if you want to make a person schizophrenic, always be inconsistent and change the way you treat them, without letting them know what is coming next. This is our current media, one day they are saying something is true, the next day it gets changed to being false. It's difficult to determine on a regular basis what is true and what is false.

The people in families we utilized for truth and role models in the past have changed drastically in the past 50 years. Families are not as intact as they once were. In 2014–18, the share of families headed by single parents was 75% among African American families, 58% among Hispanic families, 37% among white families and 21% among Asian families. One can see how difficult it is in 2020 to learn how to successfully meet our needs in a reasonable manner. That is why so many people have difficulty choosing healthy behaviors to meet their needs that they are driven to meet in a way that would normally be contrary to their belief system or moral compass.

This brings us to how people meet their needs in destructive gangs. The need for belonging is fulfilled by other gang members, since the person becomes an integrated part of a group with a common philosophy.

Their need for achievement and power is met when they cause destruction to property or people. In primitive societies, killing or imprisoning/dominating a person was and still is one of the most intensive ways of meeting the need for sick, unhealthy power (taking everything a person values, including their life). Therefore, the people who riot and hurt and kill people and cause multiple damage, by burning others or their possessions, are meeting their need for power to the extreme. There are people who pay gangs to do their bidding, as well as the money gangs extort from people, all enhancing their need for power.

In contrast, a healthy person meets their achievement or power need most intensively by talking to groups of people and having them listen, via performers, politicians, teachers, etc.

The need for freedom is met by a gang member in unlawful activities that law-abiding citizens can't and won't perform. If a gang member doesn't experience the natural consequences of being arrested for unlawful activities, they will be free to continue their unlawful behavior. This is a very powerful way of meeting their intrinsic need for freedom, which lacks boundaries.

As sick as it sounds, a gang member has their need for fun met intensively by adrenaline-producing destructive behavior as well as through, most often, brain-altering illegal drugs.

Because a gang member meets their psychological needs as intensively as they do as a gang member, it is very difficult to rehabilitate them to meet their needs in a healthy, productive manner, especially when movies and other media promote destructive scenes.

Chapter 19

COVID-19 Vaccine Injury

Information from DOD data

My media go-to for information to determine if COVID-19 vaccines are causing miscarriages, cancer, and neurological disorders among Military, is the DOD data.

Since I am a former Army Psychologist and have over 55 years in the health field, I feel it is my responsibility to report on the below government hearings, to as many in the military and civilian communities as possible. As I did in 2010, I personally persuaded the US Congress to hold hearings on the relationship between suicide and psychiatric medications. That is why I only desire that Sen. Ron Johnson's hearings, described below, can provide information that will protect the health of our military and civilian communities.

Please read what has come out in these hearings, since it may have a direct impact on you and your family. When you do, ask yourself, "Who has been preventing me from obtaining this information in the past and what do they have to gain?"

January 26, 2022, *Covid Vaccines Causing Miscarriages, Cancer, and Neurological Disorders Among Military, DOD Data Show.*

"Attorney Thomas Renz on Monday told a panel of experts that data provided to him by three whistleblowers show COVID-19 vaccines are causing catastrophic harm to members of the US military while not preventing them from getting the virus." (T*he definition of a vaccine is to prevent a disease—this is not the case here*).

Following Monday's panel discussion on COVID-19 vaccines and treatment protocols, led by Sen. Ron Johnson (R-Wis.), Renz summarized data obtained from the Defense Medical Epidemiology Database (DMED), the military's longstanding epidemiological database of service members.

The data shows:

- Miscarriages increased 300% in 2021 over the previous five-year average.
- Cancer increased 300% in 2021 over the previous five-year average.
- Neurological disorders increased 1,000% in 2021 over the past five-year average, increasing from 82,000 to 863,000 in one year.

The whistleblowers provided the data knowing they would face perjury charges if they submitted false statements to the court in legal cases pending against the US Department of Defense (DOD).

Renz told the panel a "trifecta of data" from the DMED, the DOD's military-civilian integrated health database, Project SALUS, along with human intelligence in the form of doctor-whistleblowers suggest the DOD and the Centers for Disease Control (CDC) and Prevention have withheld COVID-19 vaccine surveillance data since September 2021.

"Our soldiers are being experimented on, injured, and sometimes possibly killed," Renz said.

Following Renz's presentation, attorney Leigh Dundas reported evidence of the DOD doctoring data in DMED to conceal cases of myocarditis in service members vaccinated for COVID-19.

The military whistleblowers reported a DMED search of "acute myocarditis" resulted in 1,239 cases in August 2021, but the same search in January 2022 resulted in only 307 cases.

Cardiologist Dr. Peter McCollough, commenting on Renz's presentation, told the panel myocarditis is being falsely described as mild and transient when, in reality, it causes permanent heart damage and is life-limiting in most cases.

The military did not take any safeguards for the most at-risk age group for vaccine-induced myocarditis 18- to 24-year-olds.

Renz also highlighted a broader data set from Project SALUS, run by the DOD in cooperation with the Joint Artificial Intelligence Center (JAIC), which sends weekly reports to the CDC.

Project SALUS analyzed data on 5.6 million Medicare beneficiaries aged 65 or older. Data were aggregated from Humetrix, a real-time data and analytics platform that tracks healthcare outcomes.

According to Renz, the Project SALUS data as of late last year show:

"71% of new cases are in the fully vaccinated, and 60% of hospitalizations are in the fully vaccinated. This is corruption at the highest level. We need investigations. The Secretary of Defense and the CDC need to be investigated."

The Humetrix presentation summarizing the data in Project SALUS, "Effectiveness of mRNA COVID-19 vaccines against the Delta variant among

5.6M Medicare beneficiaries 65 years and older" (Sep. 28, 2021) has not been made public.

The Project SALUS report also included data on natural immunity, stating the vaccines have waning protection. The data also showed an upward trend of breakthrough cases suggesting booster shots could contribute to prolonging the pandemic.

"Breakthrough infection rates 5 to 6 months post-vaccination are twice as high as 3-4 months post-vaccination," the report said.

According to the Humetrix overview of the Project SALUS data, Congress must investigate vaccine failure, along with increased risk reported for breakthrough cases (or vaccine failure) in North American Natives, Hispanics, Blacks, and males.

People with kidney disease, liver disease, heart disease, and cancer treatment, along with people over age 75, are the most likely to experience breakthrough cases, while medical authorities advocate vaccines to these same populations to allegedly "protect the vulnerable."

Project Salus reported the vaccines were only 41% effective. This low level of infection prevention needs to be analyzed against the counterweight of a threefold to tenfold increase in chronic disease signaled in DMED.

The US Food and Drug Administration (FDA) requires only two adequate and controlled studies to approve a biologic, even if those studies are industry-sponsored.

The FDA now has data from the entirety of 3 million people employed by the DOD and 5 million people in Medicare. This data serves as independent substantiation that scientific fraud has occurred.

Based on this data, the FDA must revoke the Emergency Use Authorization for the Moderna, Pfizer, and Johnson & Johnson COVID-19 vaccines, and the Biologics License Application for Pfizer's Comirnaty vaccine.

It would be wrong for the FDA to extrapolate the industry's clinical trial data to pediatrics without halting the use of the vaccines and conducting an investigation based on this real-world data.

- Watch Renz's testimony here: https://rumble.com/vt7f7z-attorney-thomas-renz-statement-on-dod-whistleblowers-findings.html

- Attorney Thomas Renz — Statement on DoD whistleblowers findings https://childrenshealthdefense.org/defender/covid-vaccine-mandate-pilots-violates-federal-law-passengers-risk/

After reading the information above, it is shocking that the media in the United States has not provided front-page headlines with the above information. Now ask yourself how the TRIAD I mentioned previously benefits from not allowing a free press to do its duty in a democracy. My answer to this question is, POWER AND MONEY. ❖

Bart P. Billings, Ph.D.

About the Author

Dr. Bart P. Billings has been working in the fields of Mental Health, Human Services, and Management for over 55 years. He has possessed licenses in Clinical Psychology, Marriage, and Family Therapy, Pupil Personnel, Certified Rehabilitation Counseling (Received the Elkins Award, 1972, from The National Rehabilitation Counseling Association, Counselor of the Year for the State of California) and has an extensive background in management and program development. In Feb.2014, he received the International Human Rights Award from the Citizens Commission on Human Rights (CCHR). On June 3, 2016, the University of Scranton (where Dr. Billings received his BS and MS degrees), presented him the Jesuit University's highest award, the Frank O'Hara Award, given for living the Jesuit values of Serving Others over his career.

Dr. Billings holds a PhD in Research and Program Development, as well as a PhD in Psychology, from Saybrook University. In 1974, his text, The Development of a Transitional Rehabilitation *Program for Mentally Ill Offenders*, was published by Free Person Press/San Francisco, CA. As Chief of Professional Services/Assistant Director in the Teaching Hospital's Physical Medicine & Rehabilitation Department (PM&R) at the University of California, Davis (UCD) Teaching Hospital, Dr. Billings was initially hired as chief psychologist in PM&R to oversee the Psycho-Social-Vocational section, and after 9 months was promoted to oversee all sections (PT, OT, Speech, Psycho-Social Vocational, Orthotics-Prosthetics, Out-Patient nursing, etc.) in the PM&R hospital department.

He also founded the Institute for Occupational Services (IOS) and was the Commanding Officer for an Army Reserve General Hospital Section. With thirty-six years of service in the US Army as enlisted and as an officer, his highest military rank was Colonel (SCNG-SC Medical Directorate). Dr. Billings founded and directed: The Annual International Military and Civilian Combat Stress Conferences (24 yrs.), Prisoner of War Conferences, and the Human Assistance Rapid Response Team (HARRT), which was accepted at the Pentagon in 1997 as a readiness protocol to be implemented military wide.

National and international documentaries, TV news shows, and extensive radio shows, including HBO's Vice News (previously ABC's Night Line) and US News and World Report, have featured Dr. Billings as a guest discussing Combat Stress. Congressional and State Legislative Hearings have heard testimony from Dr. Billings on the need for better Mental Health Treatment Programs for military personnel and their families. Some of these hearings resulted in the awarding of a multi-million-dollar Department of Defense grants for national research on how to improve treatment for Post-Traumatic Stress Disorder and Traumatic Brain Injuries. Congressional Hearings held on Feb. 24, 2010, were initiated by Dr. Billings, who provided testimony on the relationship between psychiatric medication and increased suicides in the military (available on the Congressional Record). In September 2012, he lectured to the psychology faculty at West Point Army Military Academy.

On June 5, 2003, he was named as a member of the Governor's Advisory Board to Patton State Hospital, California, and has worked overseeing all psychological services for the San Diego District of the California Department of Rehabilitation (DOR). Also, while at DOR he functioned as a Rehabilitation Counselor Supervisor and Staff Development Coordinator for Northern California Region. He has developed residential treatment programs in substance abuse and alcoholism, as well as human assistance programs for the civilian and military community. Recently, Dr. Billings wrote a chapter in a book for attorneys called, *Attorneys Guide to Defending Veterans in Criminal Court*. He is a member of the National Center for Youth Law Medical and Scientific Advisory Board.

Dr. Billings had been senior faculty at the William Glasser, MD, Institute for over thirty years and has thought classes at the University of San Francisco, University of California Davis, United States International University, and others, as well as workshops on counseling and management throughout the United States. He speaks on Health and Nutrition with the focus on *The Psychology of Eating, How We Choose to Eat–Alternative Thinking/Healthy Cooking*. As prior owner and operator of a restaurant for 4 years, he practiced his teachings.

He was the founder and president of a manufacturing company called TBH Productions that produced Omni Sonic professional audio omnidirectional loudspeakers. His work with sound and his vast experience in the medical field has resulted in him writing an article in the *Navy Medicine Journal* titled, "The Sound You Feel Can Be Dangerous to Your Health" (Jan–Feb 2002, p.22-26), which deals with Vibroacoustic Disease. He also was published in *The Hearing Journal* (August 2019, Volume 72, Number 8), "Vibroacoustic Disease: More Than a Hearing Problem". He was awarded an Honorary Chaplain Certificate from the Georgia State Defense Force.

For over thirty years, in his spare time, Dr. Billings has volunteered for charities as a performing art — special events director, producer, and writer. One of the shows he is most proud of writing and producing was, *Good Grief It's Lucy*, (for the International Missing Children's Foundation), collaborating with the producers of the TV Peanuts series producers ,who contributed seven original songs for the show. He has directed The *All-American Festival*, which raised funds for Veterans Scholarships. From April 2008 until November 17, 2012, he personally owned a very popular restaurant/bar in La Costa California, drawing many retired and active-duty veterans, who often spoke to Dr. Billings about their own personal issues with combat stress problems. The restaurant catered for hundreds of events in the local community as well as at the Camp Pendleton Marine Base. One event there was for the Department of Defense Secretary's visit, with 500 guests being personally served by the restaurant staff. Even before covid, Dr. Billings had a strict policy that at all catering events, he had his staff serve every single guest personally. An article in the military section of the *North Coast Times* (9-17-10) described his work with veterans and their visits to his restaurant, including Officers Staff Meetings and Marine Family Dining. In the 2018 winter issue of The Marine Corps League's *Semper Fi Magazine*, he was interviewed on Combat Stress Issues. He was also asked to be a Commissioner for the CCHR International organization. His book titled

Invisible Scars: Treating Combat Stress, PTSD Without Medication (#1 Best-Seller), covers over 40 years of his work with Combat Stress' residual effects on our veterans and their families, with the Marine Corps League distributing over 1000 copies to its members for use in peer groups.

Bart P. Billings, Ph.D.

COL SCNG-SC (Ret), Military Medical Directorate

Licensed Clinical Psychologist PSY 7656

Licensed Marriage, Family Therapist MG 4888

Director/Founder International Military & Civilian Combat Stress Conference

Initial Enlisted Ranks and Retired as Medical Service Corps Officer with a total of 34 years in US Army

Recipient of the 2014 Human Rights Award from Citizens Commission on Human Rights International—The University of Scranton "Frank O'Hara Award" in 2016

Contact Bart P. Billings, Ph.D.
bartbillings@yahoo.com

From the Library of Bart P. Billings, Ph.D.

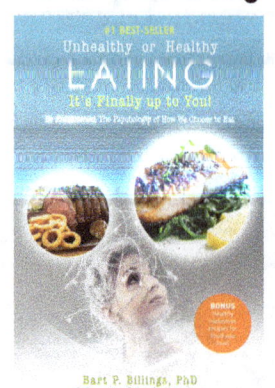

Unhealthly or Healthy Eating—It's Finally up to You!: Be Enlightened: The Psychology of How We Choose to Eat
ISBN: 978-1937801830
Paperback $12.99 | 140 pages

If you have ever tried to lose weight only to gain it all back, this book is for you! Look and feel healthier, take control of your eating behaviors, and live a balanced an healthy life. Dr. Bart Billings, a psychologist with over 50 years of experience helping people successfully deal with the most challenging issues in their lives, shares how you can use Choice Theory Psychology to help you make the right food and nutrition choices. Break through old behaviors and limiting thoughts to make better food choices and become healthier while losing weight.

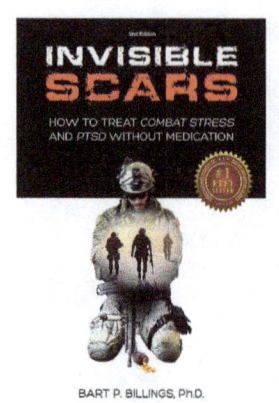

Invisible Scars: How to Treat Combat Stress and PTSD without Medication, 2nd Edition
ISBN: 978-1937801854
Paperback $17.95 | 278 pages

Everyday approximately 22 veteran suicides occur with many of them using or having used mind altering psychiatric medications, prescribed for residual effects of combat stress, such as PTSD. Unfortunately, for well over a decade, the military and VA has had a policy of treating combat related stress problems with psychiatric medications, which have a host of Black Box side effects, including suicide, homicide, anger, hostility, poor judgment, etc. Post Traumatic Stress (PTS) is a normal human reaction to what can be considered abnormal situations. The 'D' (Disorder) is added to PTS when the soldier or veteran can't return to normal functioning. In this tell all book, Dr. Billings chronicles the VA & the Military's decision to use brain/mind altering medications for residual effects of combat stress, why they do it, the effects on veterans/soldiers, and how new integrative treatment programs are now helping military veterans return to normal, healthy lives, without brain/mind altering psychiatric medications. Leading the call for a more intelligent, more effective and humane treatment is Bart P. Billings, Ph.D., a clinical psychologist, retired enlisted soldier, and Medical Service Corps officer (USA retired - 34 yrs.). He has successfully treated hundreds of soldiers with combat stress reactions and PTSD without psychiatric medications. Dr. Billings is also the Director/Founder of the International Military & Civilian Combat Stress Conference, the longest running conference of its type in the world and developer of the "Human Assistance Rapid Response Team (HARRT)" readiness program, which helps soldiers and their families prepare for the stress and challenges of deployment. The HARRT readiness questionnaire is included in this book. This book is a must read for anyone who knows or treats those with combat stress related problems, such as, PTS, PTSD, TBI.